CONTENTS

THE LEGAL STUFF

This is a work of fiction. Any & all names, corporations, businesses, organizations, charities, places, events, locations, incidents, scenarios, are either the products of the author's imagination & or used in a fictitious manner & or poorly written parody & or pastiche & or fair dealing & or fair use & or caricature & or review

Any character's resemblance to any persons, living, dead or any possible combinations between these states, is purely coincidental & or fictitious & or fair dealing & or fair use & or review, & or is poorly written parody & or pastiche & or caricature

This book contains swearing and bad language and is unsuitable for anyone under the age of consent or anyone of or above the age of consent.

This book contains fictional graphic violence, and this book contains fictional child torture and is unsuitable for anyone under the age of consent or anyone of or above the age of consent.

This book is written specifically to challenge and to be controversial. At the time of publication

This book should not be read by anybody ever under any circumstances ever ever ever

PRE-PREFACE

Logic if you knew how to think you'd be dangerous

If you already know what logic is and how it work's then you can skip this, as this is the most basic introduction to this subject.

Logic is most probably not what you have seen in the movies, nor is it what you've seen on TV.

Logic in its working application is the construction of an argument, and that's it, nothing more nothing less, it's just the construction of an argument it's as simple as that.

It is not the conclusion of an argument. (So if you hear someone say that's a logical argument, this actually means the conclusion may well be false, but hay it's a well-constructed argument kudos, although it's far more likely the person saying this is quite ignorant about logic ;-)

It is not the elements/proposition/evidence, or in correct technical terms the premise/s of an argument.

It is not the argument itself.

It's just the construction, yes I know I'm repeating myself, but this is an important point.

Let me demonstrate, by constructing a logical argument.

"Argument" a banana is fruit, a banana is yellow. Therefore all fruit is yellow

It is not a sound argument. It's a silly argument, but it is logic, and here's the breakdown, hit that cool background jazz music.

Premise "a banana is fruit" premise "a banana is yellow" conclusion “all fruit is yellow.”

The conclusion does not follow from the premises. It's a “non sequitur” or the sequence is screwy.

And the two premises I chose were inaccurate, sneaky ain't I

A banana is not necessarily yellow, it's sometimes green or black or brown as well as sometimes yellow.

A banana is not fruit.

Bananas grows from a herbaceous plant, the idea of a banana tree is a common yet inaccurate misconception, now as bananas grow from monstrous sized herbaceous walking (Look it up.) plant's this means bananas are classified as either herb's or berries, although I try to remain somewhat neutral myself, there is a heated dispute over this classification by the herbalists and berrieists, I believe this will undoubtedly eventually lead to a mighty and savage war, between these two intransigent groups that will eventually destroy all civilization, but I digress ...

So how can logic be useful in an everyday situation?

Well, if the premise/s is correct, it follows that the conclusion must be correct.

Like this “argument” all bachelors, are unmarried

There you go a logical argument and a sound argument, yippee!

And logic can be extremely useful every day in identifying the unmarried at bachelor parties

Basically, the upshot is if you nail those/that premise/s then you nailed that conclusion, although there are limitations as described later in this book.

Perhaps the greater use of knowing how an argument should be constructed, is knowing how to deconstruct an argument, and how to spot un-sound or fallacious arguments

You may wish to investigate fallacies, as I may have made some mistakes in this book.

Wink look above “herbalists and berrieists” slippery slope fal-

DAVID NORMAN WARD

lacy

PREFACE

I'm a prolific reader, and lately for whatever reason I've been blighted by a huge streak of really awful books, and I thought to myself ..... As you do ..... Hay I can write a really awful book ....so here it is.

At this point I'm supposed to set out the aims and thank those that helped.

First the latter

Special thanks to

In order of importance

Let me first congratulate myself, let's face it without me this book would not be possible, some people may consider this immodest, but let me assure you I cannot be outdone on modesty.

Honourable Mentions

Gordon howlett "Grammar NAZI;~ aNd good sparring foil thank you for your input although mostly ignore'ed ;D

Common-Law name "Dream" an inspirational synchronistic fellow whom baffles and befuddle's my more studious methodological outlook, may the last be First

The aims well it's a fictional zombie story and a bit more

Let me demonstrate something to you, just for fun I shall prove that black is white, nobody in the world has done this before.

So you should be impressed .... But you won't be, human nature can be just so predictable at times.

Like this ... choose.

<u>That way</u> or <u>This way</u>

Think about it ..... And make your choice, I'll tell you the choice you made, and why at the end of this.

Anyhow's I digress, back to proving black is white.

Caveat this is for non-luminous and non-refracting objects.

A little photon of light bounces off an object into your eye

Thus, you see and perceive that object.

The object itself appears to have colour because of this reflected light.

Should you see a yellow ball then this is because when normal ie full spectrum light hit's an object, it absorbs all but the reflected yellow light

Which means, the object itself is every colour except the reflected colour yellow

Thus, if you see a white ball then you have only seen an inverted reflection of its true colour black, therefore white is black and black is white

Caveat to myself, be very careful on the next zebra crossing

Are you impressed? .... I did tell you, you wouldn't be, people are just so predictable, and talking about predictability.

The answer to your earlier choice is ...... This way

It's a fifty/fifty choice, or was it? I did use the words "think about this" And as you wouldn't like to appear stupid especially to yourself, which may well occur if you jumped unthinking for that first answer, well this makes that second choice far more favourable.

Additionally, "This way" just sounds more comfortable, with connotations of majority thinking inclusiveness being part of the team, safety security warmth and all that fluffy hugs and bunnies stuff

Where "that way" holds connotations of the unknown, the scary

To that one person that didn't fall for this, well done... there's always one.

Anyhow's, the point of this and the aim of this book is to challenge your thinking. To bring into question some of your preconceived ideas, do you still think black is black unquestioningly?

This is an ambitious project all by itself, so why have I put zombie's in the mix, well because we are a narrative driven species, and we have a very long tradition of mixing ideas philosophy into fictional stories, for reasons that you can work out for yourself (Or I'll put in the next book, if you can't be bothered working it out yourself.) and besides, I just like zombie stories, so nerrr

Whether I have been successful in this ambition, well that's up to you to judge, that is it's your choice it's your decision;-D

You have been suitably told and warned

Abandon all hope ye who reads on

CHAPTER ONE, SETTING THE SCENE

The doors burst open at full run *D*'s black formal shoes slide on the marble floor *A*'s sparkling silver heels also hold no traction *D*'s breakdancing youth allow him to keep balance turn mid slide and to go down on one knee as he catches *A*'s slender frame just as she starts to topple over.

The desk clerk is impressed and wishes he had his saiokphone ready, that entrance would have made a viral vid

D stands up still holding *A* by her waist a diminutive woman in her late-twenties now being held aloft by a silver-haired six foot tall gorilla in a black suit she curses in French and repeatedly strikes *D*'s face and chest not with force but exasperation anguish *D* in a deep slow voice says your fine as he stands her on the floor, she staggers towards the twenty-something dark haired blue waist-coated desk clerk, and she starts babbling nonsensical French at the desk clerk

D heads towards the street doors through which they both entered moments earlier, *D* swings the street doors back open

The desk clerk is watching *D* as he reaches for an old style vintage nineteen sixty's wired desk phone to call the police, but he stops himself midway as he hears the noise.

It sounds like a sporting event with a very large enthusiastic crowd in the distance mingled with car alarms and it was getting louder.

D turned his head towards the clerk and in a loud deep and measured voice he says it's heading this way, he emphasises the word NOW! He then asks is there any way of locking these doors?

The confused desk clerk stood motionless as *A* from the front of the desk is reaching clawing pawing for the desk clerk frantically pleading encouraging him to act in haste, she is shouting babbling oui yes des portes door doors lock them lock them you lock, in the not so distant background an explosion shocks the desk clerk into action and he runs over to *D* with the door keys in hand he fumbles handshaking with adrenaline

D takes the keys, and the sturdy decorative old wooden doors are locked and they rattle as *D* test's them, the desk clerk asks what the fuck? *D* say's no time... No time

D then turns his head to survey their surroundings the desk clerk name badge reads Jonathan miles under a small corporate logo saying Co'llation Ltd executive securely linked conference suites, the reception desk is garnished with green leather and some brochures repeating the logo there were also papers and the usual kind of paraphernalia one might find in a precomputer lobby, behind the desk, a solid looking wall and a backroom door the wall was garnished with health and safety notices certificates and an image of a phone with a crossed red circle and the words “phone and network signal blocking” and some smaller words not quite visible from the distance of the doorway

D continued to look around on either side of the room there were twin curved wooden staircase’s, curving back and above the reception desk to some elaborately decorated wooden railings, on the right-hand side of the staircases there was a stair lift, there was an old umbrella/coat stand with an assortment of umbrellas within it located beside the street doors, this building looked old solid and well maintained the smell of leather and cedar oil is present, formerly a gentleman's club or some kind of merchant house *D* surmised

D snapped his attention back to John and he asks which room has the sturdiest door? While waiting for the answer *D* wedged the umbrella/coat stand against the doors

Adrenaline had dried John's throat he spurted coughed and pointed to the left-hand staircase.

A was now behind the desk a pair of fixed wide open brown eyes some fingers and beaded hair were all that were visible *D* gently grabbed John's pointing arm and started to lead him up the stairs, *D* started to ask is anybody else here ?.... but before he finished THUD

The doors shook as a low-pitched groan emanated from outside and a high-pitched yelp from *A* as she disappeared behind the desk then reappeared at the side of the desk as more and more thuds and groans occurred

D raised one leg and pointed to his shoe and then held one finger to his lips *A*'s wide open eyes followed *D*'s gestures then she nodded.

D whispered to John fearless Amazonian warrior queen ha, she goes to pieces over the slightest zombie apocalypse yes, John said zombie! *D* said never mind, then he again asked is there anybody else here? As he continued to lead John up the stairs and as *A* scurried past them shoes in hand, John in a croaky voice said party of twelve running late and two cleaners from the agency

D and John reached the top of the stairs and a cleaning trolley became visible halfway down a long corridor next to an open door, *D* asked John the strongest door? John pointed towards the far end of the corridor, *D* stuck his head around the open door next to the cleaning trolley, and he saw fourteen people peering out of the windows onto the unfolding pandemonium on the streets

D let out a short whistle which got everybody's attention and caused a gasp of alarm from some *D* gestured comehither repeatedly and he also held one finger to his lips, the two uniformed cleaners came over immediately.

D quietly said, good; then turning to John he asked could you get these two and the trolley behind that sturdy door? John nodded and led them and their equipment away.

D turned back and repeated the comehither gesture to the others, while *D* softly to himself said that should stop them playing twenty questions with the desk clerk in the hallway, now come on just follow and stop advertising yourself to the infected horde below

An elderly lady in a green tweed dress and jacket with tied back grey hair and comfortable looking brown shoes, took a tentative step towards *D* stopped and looked back to the others

D smiled and nodded and continued to gesture, the tweeded lady slowly hesitantly walked towards *D* followed by several others, the tweeded lady made it to the threshold of the door to the corridor, with a reassuring hand on her shoulder *D* pointed towards the end of the corridor and said this way quickly and quietly yes, the tweeded lady nodded and moved along the corridor occasionally nervously looking backwards.

While the others formed an orderly queue and were filing out *D* entered the room to make sure there were no stragglers

The room itself was relatively large with a horseshoe shaped table pointed towards a large monitor screen the monitor showed an image of a similarly furnish yet distinctly different room full of suits, a just noticeable digitally clipped voice with a Canadian accent said who are you and what's going on? *D* said to the suit at the other location, thee apocalypse, find safety now, ask questions later yes

While the suit was starting to remonstrate *D* hit a well labelled mute button on the desk which cut the audio and simultaneously blurred the image, *D* noted that almost all the party at his location were moving towards the door, and then moving along the corridor following the old lady, the exception was a young man in a shiny grey suit, grey and black two tone brogue shoes and a slightly spiky haircut, with his back to the window the young man was reaching towards the inside breast pocket of his jacket *D* started purposely towards him

The young man pulled a phone out of his pocket and was starting to hold it up for a selfie with the infected in the background.

D closed the distance and snatched the phone out of the young man's hand with force *D* glanced at the phone's settings flash enabled, *D* crushed the phone in his hand the sound of high-pitched components and materials giving way under pressure was unmistakable, the young man in an Eaton school accents said now hang on! *D* looked him straight in the eye as he let the remains of the phone in his hands drop to the floor but before it hit *D*'s left-hand was on the young man's right bicep with astonishing speed *D* squeezed until he saw the glimmer of pain in the young man's eyes and said in a calm and measured tone, that should create a flight or fight response, and as you are not a fighter (*D* surmised this from the young man's puny struggling bicep) then it's time you ran to safety wouldn't you say yes?

The now red-faced young man nodded, *D* said apparently there is a strong door at the end of the corridor *D* released his grip on the young man's arm and placed his hand on his shoulder manoeuvring him towards the corridor where a line of people were waiting patiently to enter the room behind the sturdy door, *D* could hear and just about see the tweeded lady stood on the threshold of an off angled door frame questioning John the desk clerk about the chaos outside, the tweeded lady in a demanding manner asked what do you mean you don't know?

D's anger and frustration arose and his hand began to grip the young man's shoulder so hard the poor young man whimpered and then screamed and he began to collapse.

D said sorry as he straightened the young man up, a number of people had turned round to see the source of the scream as *D* said and sorry about this as well, *D* grab the young man by his shoulders and physically pushed him into the person standing in front of him saying MOVE! It was messy and there were howls of protest but it worked, the room they entered was smaller than the conference room perhaps twenty by twenty feet with two doors at the far wall, an inexpensive laminated table and orange plastic chairs one small Iron barred window with wooden hinged opened shutters.

The door *D* was closing was indeed very strong two inch vertical wooden beams and two inch horizontal wooden beams iron rivets and a rotating locking wooden beam which *D* struggled to lock.

This was some kind of old strong room the off angle door looked like it was designed to prevent the use of a battering ram.

D walked over to the table as the group backed away from him nervously he then flipped over the table and wedged it against the door and the floor at a forty-degree angle, he turned around and sat and then laid down on the upturned wedged table then he in a sardonic tone to the ceiling said you're welcome

The room was silent and all eyes were on *D* as he said how you doing *A*? She replied comment penses-tu toi great lumbering roast beef eating anglais, *D* laughed and said, I love you too sweetness, excuse me said a lady you have assaulted this man and destroyed his property *D* looked over to see the young man with the Eaton accent now with red eyes being comforted by a middle aged lady in a dark grey matching skirt and jacket pointed toe kitten heels and a bob haircut, *D* said I certainly did *D* then looked over to the far wall towards the two doors, he enquired what's back there *A*? *A* replied, petite chambré with some cleaning équipements and a petite cuisine no plus des door's, from what looked like the kitchen

D asked how long do you think we have? *A* replied quatre à six heures peut être *D* said that sounds about right to me, *D* then asked any ideas? *A* said, j'y travaille... je suis working on it, *D* asked John are there any rooms above us? John said just the attic I think, the middle aged lady interrupted again saying you have assaulted this man and destroyed his property! *D* enquired and your name? The middle aged lady said, Bertrice Le Fol Armin, *D* said well Bertrice the young man *D* held his hands up questioningly, Bertrice said Francis, *D* with a sideways smile said well Francis, was about to... creak scrape bang the street door caved in although the noise was somewhat muffled it was unmistakable, then running footsteps sniffing incredibly loud sniffing groans thud a body hit the door and it shuddered then a low loud groan thud, thud groan groan *D* put his hands behind his head and laid back on the table, while the group backed towards the end of the room, *D* sardonically said to the now cowering group, oh now you are prompted into action yes.

Outside the door the thuds and groans diminished although the sniffing sound increased then decreased slowly.

D said to the cowering group they are caught in a bottleneck and are crushing each other to a standstill, we are safe for the moment yes, some time passed and then the group began murmuring and whispering in frightened tones

D asked is there any coffee back there *A*? *A* sharply replied faisle toi-même *D* said hay I'm working here and it is your turn anyway's, *A* replied sat on your fat arss working and the purchase of café at cafés does not count the same as doing, *D* replied of course it does... symbolically emblematically kind-of-ish I think, a moon faced man brown thinning hair brown tweed suit with mustard yellow elbow patches and brown suede shoes whom had regained some of his composure, said hang on with all that is going on your arguing about who makes the coffee... He demanded, who are you and what's going on here?

D repeated what's going on here? Then *D* said I'm trying to get some coffee my name is *D* I'm an itinerant worker and amateur philosopher, and the prodigy she's called *A*, she's a professional mathematician with more qualification's than I can remember and she is also a gourmet coffee maker, as for the rest you can work it out for your Zen as you have seen as much as me yes, oh with the exception of the magnetic pole shift you probably won't know about that

The old lady in tweed corrected *D* by saying work it out for yourself, then she said, and the desk clerk mentioned zombies, the word zombies circulated in whisper's and tut's of disbelief

D asked the old lady in tweed, English teacher? The old lady in tweed said professor of linguistics; I'm Doctor Eva Haendale, then she smiled in a well-rehearsed manner.

D said grammar Nazi, if I survive this and if there is a time machine at the LHC then I'll go back and write me-Zen a book that will just aggravate the hell out of every grammar Nazi what reads it, there was the sound of a kicked cupboard from the kitchen and then the word merde and the sound of a metal spoon bouncing off a ceramic cup *A* entered the room smiling cup in hand, *A* said coffee my dear to *D* then she said I've just have the most merveilleux idée we should head for le ghrand collisionneur de hadrons, *D* said oh ? *A* said oui, then she asked while handing the cup to *D* and why would a grammar Nazi read your dérangé scribblings? *D* said good point...then *D* said I'll have to think on that, then he smiled sheepishly

While the group pulled out their mobile phones and where trying unsuccessfully to connect to a network

D turned to Eva and said as a professor of linguistics you should know the evolutionary fluidic bastardize poetic German language aka English is not helped but in fact hindered in its evolutionary process by grammar Nazi's, *D* continued almost to himself saying, we're just monkey's grunting at each other in an abstract language with abstract rules, oh but there's always somebody that thinks this or that should be the divine law, and they should be its self-appointed evangelical proselytizing zealot priestess and inquisitor, Eva said philosophical dictionaries ? *D* said oh now wait a sec, we are conversing in the vulgar tongue you know fu... *D* was stopped by a sharp kick to the foot by *A*, whom said THE NOW!

D said we have several maybe four to six hours yes, and then *D* shrugged his shoulders, *A* said tell them, *D* said I have already, *A* said and how would you décrire these people intellectuellement, *D* in an offhand manner said, I haven't talked to them all yet, *A* said humour me, *D* said well they were all mindless enough to stand in front of a window advertising themselves to thee infected, I'll assume although assumption is the mother of all mistakes that there is a high percentage of academic's here, so mindless academic minions might be an appropriate intellectual description, assuming my assumption is correct yes, then *D* smiled somewhat mockingly

The moon faced man appeared to take great umbrage to this and in an almost sternly manner said Stephen Hawking pronounced that philosopher's had not kept up with science and their art is dead! *D* said indeed he did yes, at a corporate symposium for laughably dull ideas and sound bite propaganda many years ago, *D* asked and your name is? The moon faced man replied Henry Burdale Stokes *D* asked physicist? Henry slightly bemused said yes, *D* nodded courteously to *A* and *A* nodded courteously to *D* then *D* grinned like a Cheshire cat, as *A* rolled her eyes as she turned to collect her own coffee.

D asked Henry been a scientist long? Henry proudly said over thirty years, *D* asked and what specifically is science? Henry said well now, that's not an easy question to answer simply, *D* said yes it is... Two words in Latin or five in English sciences the very subject you've been studying for over thirty years what is it specifically... Although what should be more self-evidently relevant to you is why don't you know?

Henry was silent his head was down, *D* said of course you're a veteran scientist you couldn't possibly admit not knowing something as fundamentally relevant to your profession as this could you yes... let me help, then *D* looked to the group which had spread out and most of them had stopped playing with their phones once John the desk clerk had reminded them that the secure conference suites meant that Wi-Fi and networks were blocked and could not be unblocked *D* asked are there any scientists here don't be shy just raise your hand.

The eyes of the group fell upon three people, *D* said good old human nature, then *D* made eye contact with the individuals, and he said and whom do we have here yes, before they had a chance to fully raise their hands, with the eyes of the group on them they felt pressured into saying, John Runndolf chemist, George Mendel geneticist, Ellicott Lestour climatologist

D asked can you help Henry out here. Yes... No? There was silence which Eva broke by saying you shouldn't shame them like this, *D* said only by admitting our own ignorance can we learn yes, although I seriously doubt I'll get an admittance of ignorance from this lot, let me help dispel some of your unadmitted ignorance, science is Philosophiæ Naturalis or in English the philosophical examination of nature, that is to say science is philosophy, the logic used in science oh that's philosophy scientific methodology oh my Isn't that philosophy as well yes ? And so on, yet you and the late Hawking's thought that philosophers had not kept up with science and their art was dead? Now that's a shameful indictment of our educational system yes, tick this box to become a scientist no innate curiosity or desire of knowledge for knowledge sake required, *D* shook his head despondently

D continued to say, anyway's I've been asked by *A* to explain what is happening please interrupt me and ask questions, let's not die of ignorance here yes

Eva interrupted and said *A* and *D*?

D said that's not entirely relevant now perhaps later, and then *D* continued to say, the infected I know nothing more about them than you, the explosions we heard and the smoke we saw, are now or are becoming raging fire's, that will not be put out by captain snout and his fire brigade I think yes, and will in all likelihood spread here giving us a limited time in this location before we all die horribly, the Earth is currently undergoing a magnetic pole reversal, which tends to happen periodically on a hundreds of thousands year's timescale, and this is happening right now, and in all likelihood this will result in a drastically reduced lifespan probable madness and death, the destruction of virtually all electronic equipment not held within a Faraday cage, dramatic sea level rise, increased volcanic activity including supervolcanoes basically the end of civilisation as we know it.

All eyes turned to Ellicott the climatologist who looked awkward and out of place in his dark green suit dark purple waistcoat and ginger Victorian style moustache, *D* smiling said this should be fun

Ellicott defensively said, so you're a climate change denier? *D* pulled a large metal e-cigarette/pipe out of his pocket which produced a custard smelling steam, Bertrice said do you mind, *D* said not in the slightest, then he continued by repeating "so you're a climate change denier?" then *D* puffed another cloud of steam and said now that's an old loaded question and loaded with old fallacies yes, why spout this kind of bullshit unless you're trying to make yourself look like either an ignorant parrot or a wilfully ignorant bullshit merchant? Ellicott said nothing.

D said well perhaps that's a false dichotomy, anyhow's let me try to rephrase it into an honest question. Am I an anthropogenic climate change the end is nigh sceptic? *D* paused and puffed another cloud of steam with rings, then said perhaps not quite as snappy adversarial accusative well poisoning or lacking in any coherent accuracy as your old phrase, but does it get the message across, was that what you wanted to ask me?

Ellicott with a stern face said yes.

D said well I always try to reserve equal scepticism for any claim, as paradigm shifts do happen yes, that being said, every action has an opposite an equal reaction and we are a part of the ecosystem, thus we must affect that system, although we are not the most prolific genus on this planet by numbers or bio mass or effect on the atmosphere, that would be bacterial or fungal or perhaps algae viridiplantae what do you think Ellicott?

Ellicott said so man made CO two causes climate change and it's the greatest threat to this planet.

D smiling said indeed and I was under the deluded belief that this planet was rather large and quite difficult to destroy, even if a not so distant supernova shockwave ripped the atmosphere off this planet, the planet itself would still be here.

Ellicott said so that wasn't what I meant.

D said indeed repeating inaccurate ambiguous jingoistic hypergandaphrases will do that yes, *D* after puffing another cloud of steam continued to say, the greatest threat to our civilisation has always been a pandemic I think, as is demonstrated by what's on the other side of that door yes, and at a guess I would have put war, a big ass'ed solar flare, an ELE meteor impact and super volcanoes up there as well as

Ellicott interrupted so super volcanoes you said that before that is just mad

D said just good old classical physics and methodological logic in this particular scenario, the Sun that rather large natural fusion reactor that can burn your skin on a nice day, it puts out a lot of energy

Ellicott said so that energy is fixed unchanging in any significant way

D said if you only count luminosity as the Suns output in energy, unfortunately the Sun itself has not read your blinkered remit of what it should and shouldn't do, so in reality there are big ass'ed solar flares, and all kinds of fun and funky stuff exploding out of the Sun, and there is also the maunder minimum maximum and other suspected but not yet known periodic solar cycles, affecting the aurora Borealis, radio communication and there is a direct and measurable correlation shown between the Sun's activity and the intensity of electromagnetic thunderstorm's and so on, we as in this planet are a boiling cauldron of magma just under four thousand miles deep, topped by a very thin crust, that is the surface we live on is only between twenty and thirty miles deep, with magma pockets from super volcanoes much closer to the surface, the earth's powerful magnetic field diverts most of the non-luminescent energy harmlessly around this planet, but with the earth's magnetic field about to go bye bye, it's introducing energy into a high energy system it's like sticking a weasel into a microwave, thermal dynamics one oh one, the weasel will go pop yes

Ellicott said so the earth's magnetic field is about to go bye bye what evidence do you have for this? Henry said yes why should we believe you?

D said good there is hope for you yet unless you have a pacemaker yes, *D* pulled a credit card size clear plastic map reading compass out of his pocket and handed it to Henry

Henry looked at the needle moving slowly and rhythmically a few degrees from side to side, then he said so what is this supposed to mean? Henry gestured with the compass *D* nodded and the compass was handed round and inspected

D said the undeniably real for those of you that know how you may wish to access the compass app on your phones to verify this, some of the group did

Francis said you destroyed my phone, and you will pay for that, *D* pulled his-wallet out of his pocket and threw it at Francis, which Francis caught *D* said my pin number is zero one zero one *D* nodded towards the door and said although money has just become meaningless, and phone's like all electrically based equipment including bioelectric carbon based life forms that's you and me will have an extremely limited life expectancy yes.

Francis threw the wallet to the floor in a petulant manner and looked away arms folded.

D said to Henry, what it means is the magnetic pole is shifting which in itself is not too surprising this happens all the time, although not so fast or dramatically that you can see it happening right in front of your eyes yes, *D* paused for a moment then continued to say, the mathematicians say (*D* pointing with his thumb towards *A*) the magnetic pole flip is happening now, meaning the magnetic field itself will collapse for a time and then re-emerge inverted

George the geneticist said, so we get new compasses, there are more immediate and pressing matters at hand, *D* said to George, remember the failed Mars mission, where everybody died yes, George said yes but they died of radiation poisoning not flipping magnetic fields everybody knows that, *D* said they died because there was a fault with their shielding against the solar radiation yes, George said yes and so? *D* said and so our protection/shielding against exactly the same solar radiation that killed everybody on the Mars mission is the Earth's magnetic field which is about to go bye bye yes ... George paused put his head down closed his eyes then raising his head eyes wide open he said ho shit, *D* said ho shit Indeed

Henry was now holding the returned compass, he said but it hasn't flipped, it's just wobbling.

A Illustrated with her hands and said the oscillation is precursor of the collapse then flip, the collapse will not be total, there will be fragments magnetic bubbles that will move rapidly then realigns the field In opposition, like oscillation collapse flip oscillation stabilize this has happen many times in past, is recorded in the périodiqu geological magnetic historys, Henry said how do you know all this? *A* said I am on team that makes predictive model this is open source, open source data sets open source science project, this is project Corona Flux many of us are heading to a meeting when, then *A* pointed towards the door and said then this

Henry said pha open source is that even science? *D* said yes open source lack's the tarnish of cronyism and corruption that the old traditional peer review publications seemed to have developed, and yes It lacks the pomp and ceremony of the old institutional educational systems, that churns out pompous scientists that don't even know what science actually is yes, but despite all that yes it is science, I could talk you through the methodology if you'd like

Henry said how come I've never heard of any of this? *D* said because Henry you get washed up celebrities pogosticking in lion cages, or cronyism and corruption varnished over live by pretty vacant talking heads sponsored by the smiling mega evil corporation and thoroughly tarnished peer review magazines publishing p-hacked mostly unrepeatable unverifiable papers that not even the most corrupt and dodgy financial investment service companies will buy into, you've never got to hear of WR one oh four a wolf-rayet star that was coming to the end of its life, pointing a powerful solar system sterilising gamma ray burst seemingly right at us, it missed by a few degrees but, you never heard about it because nobody wanted you to panic, you don't hear about these things because you don't get told diddly-squat until it's too late, you know this Henry, you've known this for years yes

Henry nodded and asked so you're certain of the flip? *D* said come on Henry science doesn't deal in certainty it's the best guess with the tools available at the time, best guess is yes with a staggeringly high probability although I wish it wasn't you can check the data and methodology yourself once we get a net connection.

Henry said so what do we do? A very attractive lady in a salmon pink dress jacket and shoes said well I need to go to the toilet, Eva said me too, as some more hands went up, Henry gestured towards the lady and he introduced her as Emily a Town Councillor, *D* nodded a hello and then gestured towards a bucket on the cleaning trolley and said the small room with the cleaning equipment looks like it will suffice in this hour of need, Emily said so it's come to this, and what about the smell? *D* smiling said I'm sure the zombies will get used to it, and there should be enough cleaning products in there to fashion a crude chemical toilet yes, the bucket was unceremoniously grabbed and the door to the small room with cleaning equipment was slammed shut and an orderly queue formed

D repeated so what do we do? As he looked towards Henry then Ellicott and smiling said we can try to lower our C0 two omissions by taxing the zombies into penury, Ellicott sarcastically said so very funny, *D* turned towards Henry and in a serious manner said what do we do ? *D* turned and smiled towards *A* and then said *A* did suggest the large hadron collider, Henry said I've worked there. Yes the electromagnets but would they offer enough protection? And the power for them? And the zombies? *D* said indeed a treacherous journey with no certainty of safety at its end, of course this is down to the individual and evolutionary factors yes

Francis snorted survival of the fittest, *D* calmly said no this is not evolution, the principles of evolution are survival adaptation propagation, if your primary tool for self-education has been television then you will have no useful accurate or relevant information to offer yes, survival of the fittest pha if television's purpose was to dumb down the populace then it has worked all too well, anyhow's in this instance it's down to who can adapt to this situation yes, Francis looked to George the geneticist who nodded then Francis looked down, Henry said hang on a sec first things first we are trapped in here you know, *D* said are we?

D turned towards *A* raised an eyebrow then *D* asked are we trapped? *A* said two definite a third possible exit, *A* turned towards John the desk clerk and asked are there any hidden exits in this room? John shook his head then said not that I know of, there are rumours of secret passages but I've never seen them, *A* looked around carefully then her eyes fell upon the Iron barred window she said the obvious, Henry said that window is barred, and *A* said how old is that metal?

D said to *A*, you're English has returned, *A* flicked her head sideways the beads in her hair clanging together as she retorted in moments of stress passion or severe inebriation you always revert to your native language.

Henry said not everybody here is going to be able to fit through that window or shimmy down whatever drainpipes are available, *D* said no there not, Henry asked so what happens to them? *D* said the obvious yes, Henry said and that's that? *D* repeated and that's that, Henry said you seem a quite intelligent person, despite your looks, can you not think of some way of saving these people, *D* said nope.

Henry looked to *A*, *A* shook her head beads rattling, *D* said as I have said this is down to the individual and evolutionary factors, four billion years of evolutionary behaviour will kick in, our innate response will be to run home to the familiar la famille the family to loved ones, *A* said stop butchering thee French language, *D* smiling said French? I fought hit wuz Latin, *A* said suré la fami-llee sound vairy Latin doesn't it, *D* said well it's in the same genus of language I think or is that Greek? What's French based on *A*? *A* glared at *D* while folding her arms.

D to Henry said anyway most of those that can... Will want to go home, and that's suicidal it's also instinctual and thus understandable. No I cannot save anybody stay or go it's every man for himself and I don't rate anybody's chances including my own, *A* repeated every man for himself, *D* said it's a colloquial phrase yes narrowing his gaze, and I didn't abandon you when the mayhem started now did I, although it beggars reason why I didn't, *A* simultaneously smiling sweetly and sardonically said it's because I'm your la fami-llee your loved one, *D* said I try to love almost everybody accept politician's.

The group some of whom were quietly conversing with each other had fallen silent as they looked towards *A D* and Henry to follow their conversation.

Emily the town councillor had returned and she said, well I'm a politician were not always loved but we do get things done, now we live in a democracy we should... *D* held his hand up in motion to stop and said no we don't live in a democracy we have never lived in a democracy, Emily said I'm not sure what planet you're living on but we live in a democracy and that's a fact, *D* said we live in a parliamentary democracy which differs significantly from democracy which was introduced by the Greeks some time ago yes, we have indirect parliamentary democracy a bastardisation of the original democracy which was such a powerful force that it had to be destroyed externally by Sparta the Hellenistic empires and finally Rome yes, Emily retorted we don't have slavery the Greeks did, *D* said I simply pointed out the inaccuracy of your original statement, and although some might argue over wage slavery in our parliamentary democracy, my point is honesty and accuracy yes we won't survive this by living on your planet of fluffy inoffensive ignorance extolled as fact yes, the point you were going to make?

Emily said my point; she paused to consider her next words carefully then she said, is we should vote on what we should do next, *D* said indeed, and do you intend to vote this fat man through that skinny window? *D* used his e-cigarette to point at a morbidly obese man, the morbidly obese man pointing to himself said Zandroe, *D* nodded to Zandroe, Zandroe nodded In return

Emily said I mean there must be some alternatives, we have to do something, *D* repeated we have to do something, then *D* said that's normally politicians speak for I am going to nibble away at what little freedom you dumb plebs have left, Emily pulled a face as if to speak but said nothing, *D* then said *A* said two definite a third possible exit, the third a secret passage if it exists would most likely be smaller than the gap in the window suitable only for *A* and a few others I think with an unknown exit if any

D looked at the beamed ceiling and said the second we dig our way to the roof, although those beams are narrower than the gap through the window, and the roof would be most precarious I think yes, is this correct? *D* looked at *A*, *A* nodded the beads in her hair rattled slightly

D looking at *A*'s beaded hair while gesturing with his e-cigarette said, those will have to go, *A* now brandishing a small kitchen knife that seemed to appear from nowhere while offering *D* a narrow eyed look of disdain for having the impertinence of even thinking of such a thing said, nobody messes with thee hair, *D* smiling said arr the Amazonian warrior queen returns, *A* squatted and started to cut small amounts of fabric from the bottom of her dress that she began to tie into her hair, while Zandroe said I'm not stupid I realise my limitations and the hopelessness of this situation for me, the group was transfixed with *A* until they caught her steely gaze and then they became transfixed with their own shoes

Zandroe continued to say although I don't want to. I don't want to die, but I must accept what is, I mean even if I did get out what then? I'm so out of shape I had to use the stair lift just to get up here I can't run anywhere it is hopeless, hopeless he held his head in his hands.

D said to Emily can you think of any exits I and *A* have not covered? Emily shook her head, *D* loudly asked anybody? There was no reply until a woman in a retro white and red polka dot dress blurted, there was no need for that, there is no need for you to talk to Zandroe or anybody in here like that, you've done nothing but bully everybody here you're just a bully and you should shut up.

Henry said Daisy to *D* as he rolled his eyes upwards *D* smiled and repeated the gesture.

D to Daisy said did I save your life by bullying you in here? Daisy said yes, but there's no need to talk to us like this no-need now shut up just shut up.

D said so for future reference I should just let you die without saying a word yes? Daisy said yes... no just don't talk to us like we're all idiots, *D* raised his hand to his glasses lowered them slightly as to look over them at Daisy revealing his large strange eyes while *D*'s gaze looked straight through Daisy, Daisy began to blush and looked away as *D* then said whatever.

Two people had been trying unsuccessfully to remove the

metal bars from the window; one of them called over to *A* and said I thought you said these would come out easily.

A looked up from tying strands of dress into her hair at the person talking, then she looked over to *D* and motioned with her head towards the window, *D* feigned an expression of ignorance, *A* quickly repeated the gesture twice, *D* rolled his eyes and shrugged his shoulders then motioned to get up but stopped himself he then turned reaching for the now mostly empty cup of coffee which he offered with feigned submission to *A*, *A* snatched the cup rolled her eyes shrugged her shoulders stood up and headed for the kitchen, while *D* stood up and lazily swaggered towards the window the group cut a path for him

D said look away and cover your eyes some did some didn't as *D* grabbed the metal bar the two people had been trying unsuccessfully to remove with his left hand and walk back to his original position holding the now bent metal bar in hand, *D* had paused slightly when walking backwards and there was a small explosion of masonry metal fragments and glass, but there seemed to be no great effort on *D*'s part removing the metal bar, *D* sat back on the wedged table and straightened the metal bar using his legs as a brace, there was a deafening silence as all eyes fell upon *D*, *D* in way of explanation for his strength said, I've worked as a labour on construction sites

One of the two that had been trying to remove the metal bar said we weakened it, then he said err could you remove the others? *D* inquired and you are? Oh I'm James Rousseau Peirce, said James pointing to himself, I lecture on logic, a slightly chubby man in an ill-fitting brown suit and almost comical tie, I'm Karl like said Karl one of the cleaners in a cleaning uniform raising his hand tentatively, then Karl a young man with pattern shaved into his hair and a well funky pair of trainers while pointing at a young lady also in a cleaning uniform said this is Junia like

Julia a young blonde lady with a Slavic accent said to *D* your shoelaces are untied, *D* said I do it to annoy grumpy old people, does it work? Junia tilted her head to one side and sharply said very funny.

D to James and Karl said I think removing all the bars at this point is a bad idea, the zombies seemed to work off sent if we wait until the smoke is dense enough to hide our sent we should stand a better chance yes, if we drop out one by one before then we could be just laying breadcrumbs for them yes *D* asked is this reasonable?

Julia said you know it is before you asked so why ask? *D* said because this is how reason works, you cannot be sure of your own reasoning as you cannot be sure of your own sanity, it requires the confirmation of others yes

Julia said I'm not sure of your sanity, *D* said then you are not sure of my reasoning. As they are one and the same yes, and as you said “you know it is before you asked” this implies you are sure of my sanity yes, you are studying psychology?

Julia with a puzzled expression said yes.

D handed Zandroe the straighten metal bar, while Junia said It's part of my paediatric nursing course, *D* said to Zandroe tap this against the walls if the sound is flat move on if there's an echo then it could be a secret passage move very slowly and very carefully yes, Zandroe moved himself awkwardly towards the back wall and a rhythmic tapping sound began, *D* stood up and swaggered towards the barred window, Junia asked *D* how did you know? *D* grabbed hold of another metal bar and said I didn't know, which is why I asked it was a mixture of assumption and reasoning.

James, the teacher of logic raising an eyebrow said, deductive reasoning? *D* said cover your eyes then he removed another metal bar with a small explosion of masonry, he poked his head through the window to survey the courtyard then he swaggered back to the wedged table holding another bent metal bar in his hand, then he said to James if you are referring to the works of sir Arthur Conan Doyle wasn't that adductive reasoning yes Doyle was no logician I think, James asked are you a logician? *D* said I suppose technically I am, James said intriguing answer

D had returned to his seated position and started straightening the metal bar as Junia said you didn't answer my question how did you know? *D* said to Junia, I gave you a general rather than a specific answer, then *D* continued to say it would take several days to walk you through the minutiae, and although we have several hours to kill we don't have days to kill or perhaps live yes, Junia was about to speak again but *D* motioned her to stop, and said let me demonstrate some of the general, you have a Slavic accent yes, Junia said yes looking slightly bemused, *D* said it's a soft-er accent a touch of Nordic rather than say just harsh Russian, Junia just had an expression of curiosity but said nothing, *D* continued to say, so your country of origin is probably Lithuania or Poland and the numbers say Poland, Junia said I am polish, *D* said I think Poland is about eighty percent Catholic so there's an eighty percent chance that your Catholic, Junia slightly defensively said I am Catholic, *D* smiling said welcome to a country of heathen's and infidels, don't worry I'm not a militant atheist here to destroy your beliefs for your own good, Junia smiling slightly said I don't think you could, *D* grinning like a Cheshire cat said indeed, would you care to test that assumption?

Julia pondered for a while looking around at people conversing with each other or getting themselves teas and coffees and some were watching her, she said no, but there's more to it I mean what you do...isn't there, *D* said lots more like the subtle inflection in your voice, but this is all assumption built upon assumption it's a bad way of thinking and if you don't stop to ask is this the right direction, then you get completely lost, Junia said so can you tell what? *D* motioned her to stop and said... before you say it, they both laughed then Junia said while raising both hands In motion to stop you're making my head hurt *D* slowly said good

D to James said “intriguing answer” James said err yes so what were we talking about? *D* said “are you a logician? I suppose technically yes, intriguing answer” James, narrowing his eyes said err yes so do you like have a photographic memory? *D* said no, I can only remember conversations verbatim for five or so years, it gets a bit fuzzy after that, James said so what did you mean by technically? *D* asked how much do you know about logic? James said I teach it, *D* said ok let me ask in a different way, what is logic? James pulling up his trousers and puffing out his chest slightly while speaking in an authoritative voice said logic is the construction of an argument premise or premise's and a following conclusion, it's the... *D* was slowly shaking his head, James stop talking and copied the slow shaking head motion.

D said you are describing the application, not the definition, which is the correct principles of reasoning yes, James said well yes, if you want to be pedantic, *D* asked is logic, not a pedantic discipline? James said well yes.

D asked could you tell me what you teach about Kurt Gödel incompleteness theorem. James said the incompleteness theorem is not really relevant to my students it's a mathematical foible I teach formal and informal logic and of course the history of logic, Kurt Gödel is briefly covered but as this is mathematical logic, I'm sure the fellows in the mathematical departments cover this in more detail.

D was slowly shaking his head again, James said yes yes, I've heard this before, yet logic works it works demonstrably just look at computers and a logical truth remains true forever, *D* asked what have you heard James? James said well this whole thing about the incompleteness theorem's invalidating logic but it doesn't it just doesn't, *D* agreed no it doesn't, James smiled nodding his head, *D* said no it doesn't invalidate logic it just undermines and puts upper and lower limits on it, empirical reality invalidates logic, James said no

D called to Henry, Henry said yes, *D* asked Henry superposition? A single particle can be in multiple positions simultaneously, or one particle or piece of matter can be in two or more places at the same time yes, Henry said yes, *D* asked empirically confirmed? Henry said yes Australia's Griffith university and Japan's university of Tokyo empirically confirmed.

D said well empirically confirmed reality contradicts logic's principle of identity, and the law of noncontradiction, if I could shoehorn in the law of excluded middle would I win a cigar ?

James sternly said no nO NO ! Logic works demonstrably and a logical truth remains true forever, then he hit the side of his fist against the wall, there was audible movement behind the wall, James in a panic motioned stop towards the wall with the palms of his hands in a vain attempt to stop that movement, *D* said what no cigar? James looked at *D* with fear in his eyes, *D* said it's OK, but I wouldn't do that again yes, James still looked panicked.

D said shall we reason together James? James said what? *D* said shall we reason together James? Or would you rather fixate on what's out there? James said but, but, *D* said James fear and anxiety are antithetical to reason, and reason is a powerful weapon we should not be without right here right now yes, James said err yes, *D* said so calm your mind James and let us reason together.

D continued to say besides, you're frightening the natives yes, *D* look towards the now silent nervously pensive group watching them, James also looked, then he visibly composed himself and pulled his ill-fitting jacket downward slightly, then James said yes reason ... what were we talking about?

D said logic and its limits, James said is that an entirely appropriate subject right here right now? *D* smiling said real isn't it, James said very, *D* said entirely appropriate? Well arguably, we have some time to kill but we want to keep our wits sharp, so we are not unthinking panicked sheep when we make our exit yes, James said well yes, *D* said and although we can speculate about the infected and are exit strategy there are too many unknown variables to come to any sound or reasonable conclusion, James said well yes, we need more information something to go on, *D* said but were in here and out there is out there yes, and that information will only become available when we make are exit, James said well yes, then James said so let's keep our wits sharp in the meantime, *D* smiling said good idea, then *D* continued to say, so what shall we talk about the meaning of life, good and evil ? James interjected the great unknowns, *D* said well there not unknowns, James said I think I would have heard If these have been solved, *D* said only if I wanted you to hear about them, and up until now I didn't, James sceptically said well please enlighten us all

D said certainly, but first, logic and you're misunderstanding of its use yes, James said as I've said it works demonstrably and a logical truth remains true forever, *D* said but not in quantum physics the principle of identity, and the law of noncontradiction yes, James said well yes but that's quantum physics, *D* said that's empirically verified reality it's how the universe works yes, James said well yes but that's still quantum physics in the real world logic works demonstrably just look at computers

D rhetorically asked quantum computers? Then *D* continued to say fuzzy logic probabilistic logic quantum logic and so on these were invented as an attempt to try and square this circle, but it still squares and circles yes, classical logic only works in black and white and the universe is a very colourful place yes, James said yes but that's still quantum physics, *D* face-palmed and then said you James are made of particles, the floor you are standing on the earth the solar system the entire universe and everything in it, it's all particles, it's not just quantum physics it is quite literally everything including you and the very air you breathe O-two in CO-two out yes, James looked confused

D continued to say, let's turn this into a simple binary choice yes, either the entire universe is wrong by not working under the principles of logic, or logic is wrong

James said, but it works demonstrably in computers, *D* said yes it works in computers it's an incredibly useful tool but it ain't no true reflection of how the universe works therefore it ain't no universal truth yes, Eva tut tut-ed, *D* said to Eva is there owt wrong wit-me syllogism epistemology ontology tautology me-tinking ? Eva said it was more the double negative, *D* gave Eva a-look, and then said to James so we move beyond the binary choice of logic that yes it absolutely works or no it absolutely doesn't work, too it works or doesn't under certain circumstances yes

James said yes logic has limits but it does work.

D said OK so Eva loves chocolate in the morning and then in the evening she loves salty fish & chips and hates chocolate, so logic doesn't work there yes, James said well yes it doesn't work with turbulent emotions desires and so on, Eva said I always love chocolate, *D* said even when you eat so much you feel sick? Eva said that's only fleeting as she flicked the idea away with her hand, they both smiled then *D* said anyway's James there are lower limits as in quantum physics yes, James said well yes

D said the incompleteness theorem is a variation on the liars' paradox, Eva interjected liar's paradox? *D* said somebody says "I am a liar, everything I say is a lie, this statement is true" Eva paused for a moment and then said that doesn't make any sense, *D* said right it don't make no sense, Eva gave *D* a look

D said anyway's the incompleteness theorem is a variation on the liars' paradox, Gödel substitutes the "this statement is true" in whatever formalization of number theory for "this statement is unprovable" if it's unprovable, then it's true, and the formalization of whatever number theory is incomplete, if it's provable then it is false, and the formalization of whatever number theory is inconsistent

Eva said that still doesn't make any sense, *D* said for sure it's vexing and most people just don't get it, like most people just don't get that zero point nine nine nine recurring is in fact one

Eva said that's because it's not, it will always be just shy of one.

D said *A*, *A* without looking up to Eva while continuing her task said Eva what is ten divided by three? Eva said well that's three point three recurring Eva paused for a moment then said recurring again slowly

D said get it? Eva said yes, but it doesn't feel right, *D* said yet three point three recurring times three must equal ten yes, Eva said yes but it still doesn't feel right somehow

D said it's the decimal point in any calculation, you can end up with an infinite amount of numbers, or a mind boggling it would take quadrillion of years to calculate finite number behind that decimal point, and as you cannot check an infinite amount of numbers, or the universe itself would end before you had time to check a mind boggling finite number, Eva said it's incomplete or unprovable, *D* said “this statement is unprovable” it's not exactly how it works but well I think you get the general gist that there are levels of complexity that logic can't handle

James said computers seem to handle them just fine, *D* said well no, if you ask a computer to calculate an infinite number it would take an eternity yes, so computers use a floating decimal point or floating point's to keep the numbers manageable, effectively rounding up or rounding down numbers, it's a fudge and when you use fudged numbers to then calculate other fudged numbers and so on and so on and so on well then you end up with a right royal logical fubawit or diminishing returns in certainty, Eva said “fubawit” (to herself quietly and chuckled)

D said anyhow's logic has a top limit a bottom limit and side limits, it just needs a pretty little bow, James looked thoughtful

D said it's the fundamentals that escape most people with mathematics and logic although some do argue that they are separate I contend they are one and the same and they're both abstract concepts.

Henry questioningly said mathematics is an abstract concept? Then he said mathematics is universal the universe runs on mathematics, *D* asked Henry why does one plus one equal two? It's a legitimate question with a legitimate answer, Henry looked confused but didn't answer

D asked *A* for her cup and then placed both his and her cups in front of Henry, *D* said two cups to Henry, Henry said yes, *D* said but they're not the same, Henry said they look the same, *D* said but there not the same, each one is unique, as each atom in the universe is unique yes

Henry said yes, and so?

D said and so you have a unique thing and another completely unique thing, Henry said they do have certain aesthetic similarities, *D* said indeed they do from an entirely human perspective they have certain aesthetic similarities, then *D* said OK how many Henry’s are there? Henry said people with the same name as me? *D* said no you, how many of you are there? Henry said one, *D* said so despite there being any number of individuals that look like you, or that have certain aesthetic similarities to you, the only number to describe or quantify you or any other unique thing in the universe, which is everything because each atom in the universe is unique is one yes, and you can never get to two, as you can never get two Henry's yes, Henry said but it doesn't work like that, *D* said that's objective reality, that's exactly how it works objectively

D continued to say, let's with our grunting monkey language point and grunt the word group or set at thing's with certain aesthetic similarities for us monkey's, and let us grunt the word one and two and we have invented logic's set theory and mathematics simultaneously, although all we've actually done in reality is create our own abstract language out of grunt's, so we can communicate abstract concepts with each other, the unique individual thing is still a unique individual thing and remains' quite indifferent about our monkey grunting, suffice to say the universe does not run on abstract monkey grunt's, despite all of our over inflated egos telling us it should, and that we should be at the centre of the universe because we are the most important thing in it, and when our monkey grunting language dies the entirely human abstract concepts of mathematics and logic will die with us, despite are over inflated egos telling us that the universe itself must work by monkey grunt's, or that any intelligent alien species must use the same knuckle dragging monkey grunting abstract mathematical concepts to communicate as we do, even though it would be a completely alien concept to any non-knuckle dragging alien species yes, base ten mathematics that's one to ten is derived from the number of digits at the end of your monkey arms, base twenty was grunted into existence by certain cultures that didn't wear shoes, and the knuckle counting Sumerian and Babylonians gave us base sixty that's time .. Sixty minutes sixty seconds angles geometry and coordinates all knuckle dragging abstract concepts

D said so Henry the fundamentals why does one plus one equal two? Henry didn't answer.

D continued to say look we're just monkey's pointing and grunting at a universe beyond our current comprehension logic and mathematics are incredibly powerful tools that have served us well for millennia but they are starting to run out of steam yes, we need a paradigm shift for the next great leap forward, and for that paradigm shift to happen we need to understand the limitations of the tools we are currently using and invent new ones yes

Eva said you don't look or sound like a person who would know these things, where did you learn all this? *D* said well I just tend to work stuff out for me Zen yes, Eva said but not using logic? *D* said ho I use logic so much I'm often accused of logical positivism, but I ain't self-evidently, I generally prefer to use my own spin on Socratic reasoning it's more flexible and less boxed-in than the formal logical systems

James said, so you said you worked out the meaning of life?

D said ho no I didn't work it out, somebody else did that, although I don't think they or anybody else fully realised what they'd done, James said so what is it? *D* said you'll be disappointed, James said so what is it? *D* said seriously you'll be disappointed it ain't like no instant epiphany or revelation or owt, James said I don't care just tell me, *D* said well if you're sure you want to know and you are ready for that disappointment? James said yes yes just tell me!

D said well the meaning of life is really quite simple and elegant so simple and elegant everybody seems to have missed it, James exasperated said yes, *D* said the meaning of life, well the meaning of life is

Zandroe yelled I found it I found it, then he placed his hand over his mouth and then removed it exposing a childlike mischievous smile and he breathlessly quietly said I've found it, then he keeled over.

D was at his side in a flash, Zandroe said I'm OK pulling himself up with *D*'s help then Zandroe said I just need to catch my breath, *D* looked him in the eye's and saw his eye's where slightly glazed and bloodshot with tiny fatty deposits around the iris *D* helped him into a sitting position with his back to the wall,

Zandroe again said I'm OK, *D* said I seriously doubt that, Zandroe while taking laboured breath said yes I know, the doctors have given me the death sentence so many times because of my weight well you know, I just skip the four stages and move on to acceptance automatically, then he chuckled to himself, Zandroe collected himself and grinning intently said I've found it the hollow in the wall

D slowly said congratulations, Zandroe said what do I do now? *D* said I'm sure you're perfectly capable of making your own decisions, as for a suggestion I'd go with a rest for a while yes, Zandroe said yes yes but the hollow what do I do? *D* said the obvious yes, Zandroe said I'm an academic, not a practical person I don't know these things

D very slowly said really, Zandroe said there's no need for sarcasm, *D* smiling said that entirely depends upon your perspective I would have thought yes, Zandroe sardonically said ha ha, now would you help a fellow out here? *D* said certainly it would be a pleasure you just need to... hang on wait a sec what do you do? Zandroe said I'm a fitness instructor, *D* and Zandroe laughed.

D said so what did you do? Zandroe said oh no, I've seen what you do, you burst bubbles, somebody tells you what they do and you burst their bubble I'm happy in my academic bubble and I don't want you to burst it, you're like some internet troll or something in the flesh, *D* said would an internet troll box logic or talk about the fundamental nature of mathematics? Zandroe said amateur philosopher and itinerant worker? *D* said they're just titles like your job title, Zandroe said I'm guessing you've already worked that out and you're just waiting for my confirmation, *D* smiled, Zandroe said I knew it, so what are you really? *D* said a bubble burster, Zandroe said more like some kind of alien intelligence or something, *D* said I've heard that so often I'm starting to wonder myself, but as far as I know I'm just a man, Zandroe said just a man that likes to burst bubbles, *D* said I try to dedicate myself towards discovering and bursting my own bubbles, Zandroe said so why are you busting ours? *D* said mostly entertainment.

Zandroe had a confused look, *D* said look around you what do you see? Zandroe looked around he saw people queuing for the makeshift toilet, people going to the kitchen to make teas and coffees, people sat around chatting or watching them, Zandroe shrugged, then *D* said given the circumstances what would you expect to-be seeing? Zandroe thought for a while then nodded and then said entertainment, *D* smiling said mostly, then he said if you tap and score the wall between the different sounds you should be able to outline the hollow yes, Zandroe said yes, it's obvious.

John, the desk clerk, said you can't do that this is a listed building, *D* said a listed building full of zombies that will probably be burned to the ground by tomorrow. John the desk clerk said I'm just saying

Zandroe said to *D* zombies burst my bubble about zombies, *D* said let me see, *D* thought for a few moments then said these memories are more than five years old and may well be apocryphal, soz's no bubble bursting but here's what me addled synapses have

D paused and said the addled synaptic connections may well lead to digressions. OK there's fugu rubripes-puffer fish and TTX not THC, sushi voodoo witch doctors tinsel town and oh and zombie cucumber's datura metel? Or is it stramonium I'm not sure if that's devil's trumpet or devil's snare it's a bit fuzzy.

D continue to say anyhow's sushi includes the highly poisonous puffer fish which makes your tongue tingle in a thrilling way or kills you depending upon the skill of your sushi chef, if it kills you then your left by the grave for three days just in case you get better, just the right amount of poison won't kill you but will give the appearance of death that can befuddle even medical professionals. Anyhow's the highly poisonous puffer fish which was also used by African voodoo witch doctors not for sushi but to give the appearance of death for some poor victim, then after the victim had been declared dead and then buried for a while, the lack of oxygen in their coffin or whatever would cause some brain damage, then the witch doctor would dig them up, use zombie cucumbers on them just to scramble whatever brains they have left, and hay presto you have a special needs zombie stumbling around with poor hygiene and the intellect of a pot smoking television head, tinsel town added the outstretched arms and the brain eating thing to the urban legend, and there was some medical anaesthetic stuff around the TTX zombie-exe or something, there was some computer modelling that peaked my interest, oh and there's toxoplasma, half of all humans are infected with the toxoplasma parasite, it alters your brain so you really; really love cats, which may explain all those cat vid's, although correlation does not necessarily equate to causation.

Zandroe said wait is that it? *D* said correlation and bad scientific methodology? Zandroe said no, the cat thing.

D said ho zombie cats? Zandroe said yes well no, *D* said wait a sec I've still got an African witch doctor zombie sushi chef in my head, oh those synaptic connections

D said brain parasites and the zombie's out there? Zandroe said yes! *D* said yes? Zandroe encouragingly said yes, *D* said yes it could well be some kind of brain parasite there are a multitude in the natural world, viral or bacterial or a viral infected bacteria zombie bacteria, or some kind of parasitic fungus like ophiocordyceps unilateralis, the zombie ant fungus where the fungus grows out of the head of its victim, or it could be some gene splicing experiment gone wrong, George said ridiculous, *D* said so what happens to the old gene splicing equipment when the new shiny equipment comes out ? George shrugging his shoulders said how would I know that? *D* said it's sold on the net for a few quid to anybody who wants to buy it; anybody Gene splicing equipment what could possibly go wrong with that? George turned away

D turned to Zandroe and said if you ever want bubble bursting entertainment then that's me and him and a little chat about gmo's in food, anyway's the infection could be caused by owt, Zandroe said it was just an idea, *D* said keep'em coming, and then *D* said zombie cats, holding his arms out and moving them up and down, they laughed, Zandroe said I'll score out this hollow and see what we have, weren't you going to tell James the meaning of life? *D* as he moved back to his original position said oh that, it's disappointing, Zandroe said even-so I'm curious myself.

CHAPTER ONE POINT NINE NINE NINE RECURRING, THE MEANING OF LIFE

D sat back and said the meaning of life, thee meaning of life is survival adaptation propagation.

James said evolution?

D said yep.

James said well that's a disappointing non-answer.

D said is it? James said OK what am I missing here? *D* said let's define some stuff, James said sure that's what philosophers do, *D* said the word meaning, has many meanings, so let's lean more towards scientific understanding rather than some woh woh divine purpose here yes, James said sure bit of a loose definition there, and evolution still looks like a non-answer

D said let's use evolution to explain the evolution of morality.

James sceptically said morality, Junia said no morality is given to us by God through the bible, *D* and James rolled their eyes then *D* joyfully said even the holier than thou don't let your children near the priest's Roman Catholic church accepts the theory of evolution, and the theory of gravity rather than sin weighing thing's down, James giggling said naughty rock, *D* joining in said evil sinful rock, Junia said you can mock, *D* now laughing said we certainly can, James was trying to stop himself laughing by covering his mouth, speaking through his fingers he tried to say I'm sorry it's him he's a bad influence but it was somewhat jumbled

Junia sternly said you can mock all you like when ure burning in the pits of hell, for all eternity! Then she stamped her foot and folded her arms as she turned towards the wall.

James fingers could not contain the laughter, *D* was already physically rolling around, and the rest of the group had joined in the laughter. It took a while for the group to compose itself, as the infectious laughter spontaneously re-erupted.

Then James and *D* finally composed themselves and James jokingly said can evolution explain laughter? *D* said one thing at a time yes, Zandroe said no way, *D* said one thing at a time then the rest will fall into place yes, but now morality, James said morality

D said morality is an evolutionary trait, which can be defined as the interplay between self-group society and species

James slightly dismissively said would you care to define good and evil as we are talking about morality.

D said sure, the ultimate good is the Grace sacrifice, sacrificing yourself to benefit others the group society species yes

Junia without turning round said, no one can have greater love than to lay down his life for his friends, *D* said John fifteen, Junia turned round and eyed *D* suspiciously, *D* said Odin/Wodin hanged sacrificed himself on the cosmological tree Yggdrasil to be granted the knowledge of the runic alphabet, so he could pass on the knowledge to mankind yes, Wodin father of the gods and father Christmas, Jesus just didn't have those flying Nordic reindeer or the big white beard, that the kids love, this came to mind because today is Wednesday Wodin's day yes, history is resplendent with fables and tales of the heroic or Grace sacrifice, as Gandhi said "gentleness self-sacrifice and generosity are the exclusive possession of no one race or religion"

James said the Grace sacrifice may well be the pinnacle of good but this is conscious choice not some evolutionary trait.

D said mother birds and other animals sacrificing themselves to help in the survival of the offspring, you even have kamikaze bacteria like salmonella typhimurium and clostridium, individual bacteria sacrificing themselves for the greater benefit of their group, sacrifice is not uniquely human nor do you need consciousness for this evolutionary trait to function

James said if it's not a conscious choice then how can it be good or evil?

D said evil is a loaded word let's just say bad yes, James said OK if it's not a conscious choice then how can it be good or bad? *D* said are you saying good and bad are entirely subjective? James raised his hand and raised a finger from that hand and then he became caught betwixt and between.

D said the rational subjective is based upon the objective reality yes, the objective reality is survival adaptation propagation, evolution works in patterns, and DNA is the memory of those successful patterns, life began on earth about four billion years ago, or began somewhere else and then hit earth about four billion years ago, success ... survival means that DNA memory pattern continuing or are added to, failure means an end to that four billion year old DNA pattern, your personal four billion year old DNA lineage is of paramount importance, although DNA is self-replicating, individual human beings are not self-replicating, despite millennia of attempting this by certain individuals with poor eyesight and hairy palms yes, thus the group society species that are, closely associated with your own DNA patterns holds a greater collective chance of survival and adaptation and is therefore of greater importance than any one individual yes

Daisy said no, the individual is all

D asked Daisy, libertarian?

Daisy proudly said yes, *D* said principle of non-aggression? Daisy said the highest form of human behaviour.

D said so if somebody initiates violence against you or your property you can retaliate in any way you see fit?

Daisy said like I said the highest form of human behaviour, no law no government, no tax which is violence, just individuals and freedom and the principle of non-aggression it would end violence forever.

D said so if a small child kicks a ball onto your lawn, which is an act of aggression against your property, you can then retaliate by shooting that child in the face?

Daisy said nobody would do that, *D* said people eat people Daisy there's a word for it, cannibalism, and there's lots and lots of other words for the nasty things some people do yes, Daisy said so you are a statist you support institutionalised state violence against the individual ? *D* said I am for liberty, equality, fraternity, *A* raised a fist in the air and said ou mort, *D* slightly taken back by *A* looked at Daisy and said but that's a non sequitur, we were talking about the principle of non-aggression yes, now Daisy as an individual that does not believe in the initiation of violence, what exactly are you planning to do about the infected out there? Send them a strongly worded letter explaining the principles of non-violence ops no it's not non-violence is it, it's something completely different oh yes it's, non-aggression backed by the ultimate blood thirsty murderous act of violence for the slightest unintentional provocation, which you think is the highest form of human behaviour yes, *D* smiled sarcastically.

Daisy went red faced.

D continued by saying hang on a sec I bullied you in here if you had a gun would you have shot me for saving your life? Daisy sharply said yes, *D* said and thus end-if today's sermon on the addled brain swivelled eyed non-aggression principle, for saving your life you would have taken mine yes, who came up with this one dimensional unrealistic fairy-tale utopian murderous philosophy? *D* raised his hand in motion to stop, and continued to say, don't answer I already know

Daisy sarcastically said of course you do, you know everything don't you. *D* said if that was true I certainly wouldn't be here now would I.

D to James said anyhow's where were we, oh yes, the meaning of life

Daisy said I wouldn't have shot you, not really, if I had had a gun, *D* said the blade itself incites to deeds of violence, Daisy said excuse me? *D* said a quote, homer the odyssey, Daisy said ho that, *D* said just the same I'm glad you're not armed, Daisy said wouldn't we be better off, if we all had gun's? *D* said under these particular circumstance's no, Daisy said why not? *D* said there is the practical, and then he continued to say in a terrible American frontier accent, well-now Calamity Jane how many bullets do you reckon you gonna be need-ing in that there six-gun pilgrim? *D* returned to his normal-ish English accent and said, then there's splattering infected blood around this might not be a good idea yes, and then there's the ethical, but I'm sure you won't worry about that yes, Daisy smugly said I got a first in ethics, *D* said well good for you, and the educational system

D to James said anyhow's the meaning of life, morality and DNA.

Eva said to James I don't understand this why would morality and DNA be related to the meaning of life? James said morality is the holy grail of philosophy, the pinnacle the Rosetta stone, it's the question that is been pursued by the greatest philosophical minds since the birth of philosophy, it is the missing cornerstone upon which you can build true understanding and answer some of the most fundamental philosophical questions, if you can explain morality using evolution and I will assume other aspects of human behaviour, then you have de facto explained the purpose or meaning of life, Eva said the meaning of life is evolution, my that is disappointing, James said so I've been told, *D* said give the man a cookie, Bertrice said they've all been scoffed looking at Zandroe

Zandroe turned around with a sheepish grin and said enlightened selfishness, *D* said how when? Zandroe said ninja smoke, while moving his one outstretched arm slowly in front of everybody, he said nobody sees the fat man at work.

Bertrice said well I did, and you should have shared, Zandroe said would you deny a man his last meal? Bertrice quietly but sternly said you should have shared

D to James said morality, James said hang on you've defined good which I will accept tentatively but you have yet to define evil or bad, *D* said it's the mirror of the pinnacle of good the noble sacrifice yes, so that would be the ignoble sacrifice of humanity any part or all to benefit yourself, to act selfishly parasitically yes

James said and Zandroe's enlightened selfishness with the cookie's? *D* said would you have liked a cookie James? James said why yes I do like cookie's, and I am feeling peckish.

Zandroe returned to his scoring of the wall pretending not to listen.

D to James said me to, James said hardly the pinnacle of evil though, *D* said unless somebody dies later of malnutrition due to the lack of say a cookie or two yes, James said ho my yes, there's quite a few calories in those cookie's I should imagine, that could easily make a real difference later, *D* said why yes, you can just imagine some poor desperate starving soul saying a cookie a cookie my kingdom for some cookie's,

Zandroe said stop it! I did it, it was wrong I apologise to everybody, I am not the most evil person in the world, now move on.

D and James started laughing, Zandroe emphasizing the B when he said the word Bastards! Then he started laughing himself, Eva laughing herself said to *D* you are definitely a bad influence on people

James to *D* said ok it's a loose and simplistic definition of good and evil

D said Occam's razor the simplest answer is usually true yes, this is just a rationalisation of the instinctive, there's an experiment with monkey's capuchin monkey's I think, you get a monkey to complete a task for a reward a slice of cucumber, just ordinary cucumber not the zombie cucumber, and everybody's happy, until the monkey spots that another monkey is getting a better chocolate cookie treat for doing the same task, then that monkey refuses the cucumber treat and goes absolutely apey, James said an inherent sense of fair play, right and wrong

D said a baby chicken isolated from birth so it never sees another chicken, living sleeping walking on a wire mesh where no food can gather and fed from a feeder around its own head height, will still peck at the ground even though there is no ground just a wire mesh, James said and this is all genetic? *D* said the genetics is mind boggling I mean truly gigantically mind boggling, it creates and controls integrates and coordinates regulates and repairs every human cell in your body it creates the folds and structure of your brain the synaptic connections, quite literally the structure and mechanism of your conscious and subconscious thought processes yes, it controls your actions from your snakebite reflex to what enzyme to use when digesting apples, we all have four billion years' worth of preprogramed behaviour patterns in us, like the fight or flight response yes, James said every "human" cell? *D* said where a symbiotic life form, you are not alone, there're bacteria on your skin and in your body without say the bacteria in your stomach you wouldn't survive, and the bacteria ain't just a silent passenger it communicates with your brain "it's feeding time" James said so how did that get there ? *D* said you don't want to know, James said but I'm in control, I control my actions, *D* said are you? Little chubby aren't you yes, James said look who's talking

D said we both know that eating too much is unhealthy, yet we both do it yes, although we would like to consider reasoned conscious decisions, and not subconscious instinctual behaviour pattern's to be the overriding factor in that what drives our behaviour, but that just ain't true, we are both examples of the conscious decision making being subtly overridden by subconscious desires or behaviour pattern's yes, James said I suddenly feel like a bit part actor on the stage of my own life, so how much control do I actually have? *D* smiling said you have the illusion of full control, James said the illusion of?

Zandroe said so it was the bacteria that made me eat those cookies, and I'm not evil.

D said nope your still an evil bastard if somebody dies of hunger, although that's most unlikely I think yes, the desire and question both manifested themselves in your consciousness, I desire and is this the right thing to do? Your body shows your innate cognitive bias, but that ain't no real or justifiable excuse for not making the conscious mental effort to suppress those desires, for the benefit of the group yes, so you're still a selfish git for scoffing all of those cookies

George said what about the selfish gene?

D turned to George the geneticist and said what exactly do you do in genetics? George said why? Are you going to tell me how to do my own job? *D* said I know precious little about genetics and I'm always eager to learn more, perhaps you could help me, I've always had serious trouble in understanding gene transcription repair regulation and the expression of the lipogenic ligase enzyme and ribosomal, I mean I understand the functionality, I'm having trouble in understanding how this dance is choreographed I feel like I'm missing something yes, do you know if there is a real time electromagnetic field model available? George said that was not my area of expertise, *D* said so what is your area of expertise? George said blastocyst (And then waited for the what's that? Question) *D* asked stem cells or chimera? George said, and you "know precious little about genetics" *D* said it's only a passing interest and it's a very very large subject, George said ain't that the truth, its chimera, but it could have been any number of fields, how did you know? *D* said I didn't but it's where the money is yes, George nodded, *D* said a brave new world, and I don't suppose you were working on human zombie ant fungus chimera? George emphatically said no.

John Runndolf the chemist said just what were you working on George? George said I've already told you I'm under a very strict non-disclosure agreement, John Runndolf said that was then George, I think it's safe to spill the beans now, George defensively said no, it wouldn't feel right somehow, it's not something I want to talk about

Eva said why are you being so defensive George? George remained tight lipped.

Henry said why don't you come clean George? George remained silent.

D said it's because he said chimera, blastocyst is a nebulous word, chimera was a word too far yes, Eva said chimera Greek mythology lion's head, goat's body eagle wings fire-breathing, *D* said serpent's tail, slain by Bellerophon, playing god by mixing animals genetically, would you want to admit it?

George said mankind has been doing this since the stone age with selective breeding it's nothing new, *D* said well that's the public relations spin, though it ain't true is it, selective breeding of a horse and a donkey will give you an infertile jackass yes, but that's the same genus equus, selective breeding of a horse and a spider equus arachnida via genetic manipulation just didn't happen in the stone age, although as this does create a transfer point for diseases among different genus, had stone age man somehow have done this by magic, then stone age man probably would have wiped out the human-race with mad spider disease or something yes

George said that's just ridiculous, and this is all under scientific control it's all perfectly safe.

D said more public relations spin, that just ain't true yes, there is a pattern of defensive bullshit emerging here, *D* continued by saying, George are you incapable of talking honestly?

George said you wouldn't understand.

D said now there's an accidental truth yes

Eva said am I incapable of understanding George?

George remained silent.

D to Eva said I think you are incapable of understanding, although this is playing semantics yes.

Eva said I don't understand, James said neither do I

D said it's really quite simple, create a horse man alligator spider chimera in a lab and it's all perfectly safe-ish, there is the danger of creating a transfer point for diseases but as long as it's kept in a lab, then everything is hunky dory, it's controllable predictable you can make predictive models about what's going to happen, then see if those models pan out, methodological empirical science at work yes, but well in reality that just ain't so, the horse man alligator spider created by Reckless-Gene Corp is taken outside and eats genetically modified grain, created by Hubris-Gene Corp, although it's not labelled as genetically modified grain, it's labelled under its subsidiary as Healthy Natural Friendly Hugs and Bunnies grain Corp, then the horse man alligator spider gets bitten by a rogue genetically modified mosquito created by Nihilistic-Gene Corp, and the horse man alligator spider shit's genetically modified shit and wee's genetically modified wee, spreading all that genetically modified shit about, now all those modified genes created by different secretive companies that don't share information can get together and have a little party, and because these are modified genes it's an anything goes party, the natural gene protection safeguards have been bypassed and neutralised yes, those annoying natural safeguards that produce infertile jackass's can spoil all the fun yes, so you've got a mashup lad experiment gone absolutely wild in the natural environment, RNA DNA horizontal transfer and leakage into the water table, then into bacteria vegetation insects invertebrates and all the way up and down the food chain literally and eventually into every living thing on the planet, from the food we all eat to mother's milk with totally unpredictable consequences yes, now what could possibly go wrong with that?

Eva said dear god I don't understand why would you do that George?

George said it's not like that at-all, and you must understand for mankind to advance certain risks must be taken.

John Runndolf said “certain risks” what are those risks?

George said nothing and a long silence manifested, group conversations stopped and heads turned.

John Runndolf said what are those risks George?

George said I don't know I wasn't involved in anything like that.

John Runndolf said so what were you involved in specifically?

George remained silent while looking at his own shoes.

John Runndolf turn to *D* and said you can do that clever thinking stuff, what was he up to? *D* said at a guess I'd say something shameful yes beyond that I cannot say, John Runndolf said I could have told you that, *D* smiling said well then you can do that clever thinking stuff as well, when you put your mind to it yes, John Runndolf said I have my moments but I think you're in a different league to me, *D* said no, mentally there's nothing I can do that you cannot it is all within you yes, so what do you do in chemistry then?

John Runndolf was hesitant to reply his face contorting slightly with thought, *D* said is it a difficult question? John Runndolf said look I've seen what you can do, somebody gives you a scrap of information and you rip them apart with it, I do nothing shameful in my work, as he eyed George, but I don't want to be next.

D said rather bear those ills we have, than fly to others that we know not of, thus conscience does make cowards of us all. John Runndolf said what? *D* said Shakespeare hamlet to be or not to be, although to be truly appreciated it should only be recited by good old Yorkshire accented folk, as the background chatter resumed, John Runndolf said I don't understand? *D* said we'd all like to assume we'd readily embraced the light of truth, although when faced with it most shy away yes, John Runndolf said I'd like to embrace the light of truth about George and what he was up to, strict non-disclosure agreement my ass, shame more like, and to think he's godfather to my children, then John Runndolf silently narrowed his eyes on George

D quietly said the heightened emotion of the situation, and betrayal

Eva said I doubt he will confess “certain risks” with my grandchildren’s and all our grandchildren’s future, shame seems as scant regard for such reckless hubris, I thought I knew you George, you had the veneer of a decent human being

Henry told George you should stop this by admitting what you were up to.

George remained entranced with his own shoes tight-lipped controlled breathing.

D said we are in a confined space emotions are running high let's cool this down yes, then *D* said James where were we on the meaning of life?

James looking with disdain at George said, the selfish gene.

D said it can be advantageous for an individual in the short term but ultimately it is self-destructive, especially when you get found out by the group like Zandroe and the cookie's yes.

Zandroe said oi don't drag me into this.

D said I'm just trying to calm the situation down a bit, (*D* pointed with his e-pipe towards the door) what's happening may well not be genetic, and even if it is, it is highly unlikely that George was directly involved yes, Zandroe said so you're saying he may not have directly although he may well have indirectly started the apocalypse we now face, and that supposed to calm the situation down?

D moving his outstretched forearms and open hands down, said speculation without evidence is quite pointless at this point yes, Zandroe said but we all now know he was up to something dodgy it's blatantly obvious just look at him just look

D said Indeed and you all feel betrayed and that's all perfectly natural and understandable, but what are you going to do about it torture the information out of him, hold a kangaroo court? Let's all try to be reasonable yes, and let us not forget he is a geneticist and that particular skills set may well be essential for our survival later yes.

Zandroe concentrated for a moment shrugged huffed and returned to scoring the wall.

D said James where were we on the meaning of life? oh yes genetic memory and advantageous behaviour patterns

James said what?

D said just like now yes.

James said huh?

D said there is a general feeling of betrayal and anger yes, James said well yes, *D* said and George is feeling ostracised and shamefaced yes, James said well yes, and so he should, *D* said yet all he is doing is remaining silent yes, James said yes, but, but what you said and what he said

D said yet all he is doing is remaining silent yes, James hesitated for a moment then said yes, *D* said so it's emotional and not entirely reasoned, there's the general feeling of obfuscation a sense of concealment but that ain’t nothing concrete, there is a distinct absence of evidence yes, so you're reacting emotionally, the primeval sense of betrayal yes, James said well it's what makes us human

D said but you're a logician, are you admitting that you’re reasoning is being subverted by your primordial emotions and your primordial sense of morality? James rubbed his chin thoughtfully then said morality isn't fixed, different societies have different moral codes, *D* said the same societies have different moral codes overtime, we don't burn witches’ any more, evolution, James said some society's still do burn witches, *D* said less evolved societies, James said is that for us to say ? *D* said yep “evil prevails when good men remain silent” don't get sucked in to the politically correct self-censorship bollocks

Emily said it is not censorship, being thoughtful considerate and respectful of others is the way forward, and we should all be mindful about offending others, words like “less evolved” can be deeply offensive, *D* said bollocks, firstly you don't know what the word censorship actually means, you're making an argument from ignorance, secondly I find your breathing in and out deeply offensive, you should be more considerate and pander to my delicate easily offended sensibilities, and stop your deeply offensive breathing immediately yes, or shall we have a pragmatic compromise, were you breathe a lot less yes, Emily said fuck you

D said that's the correct response to any politically correct self-censorship progressive helpful inclusive sustainable bullshit, and you still don't know what censorship means

Emily said you're not as smart as you think, I know exactly what censorship means my great-grandfather was a film censor.

D said OK Emily what's the definition the etymology of the word censor then?

Emily hesitated momentarily then said so why don't you tell us all?

D said certainly it's the title given to a couple of ancient Roman magistrates

Emily's well practised political poker face slipped visibly she said no, that's not right as she turned to Eva, Eva shrugged and said nothing, *D* said they did the register or census of the roman citizens, census censor yes, and they also did the supervision of public morals. Morals that's what me and James were chatting about before you interrupted yes, Emily said morals yes my great-grandfather used to have certain scenes removed or remade for moral reasons, *D* said so censorship is about deleting stuff? Emily said yes... I think I'm not sure now, *D* said an honest politician wonders never cease, Emily said we're not all bad, some of us actually want to do some good, *D* said a good apple in a rotten barrel ? Emily said it felt like that sometimes.

D said censorship is all about exercising the control of information, it's all about control, aggressive control deleting stuff, and passive control the film makers starts censoring themselves anticipating what your great-grandfather will or will not allow, or surreptitious control a popular talk radio show vet's those that are allowed on air, via having the callers go through the show researchers vetting system, so that you only get eloquent educated people on one side, and inarticulate uneducated substance abusers on the other side of whatever agenda driven controlled argument, that's being surreptitiously pushed at the time yes, or the more insidious control, a government lets slip that their reading everybody's digital correspondents and everybody starts considering carefully exactly what they write yes, governmental inspired self-censorship on mass

Emily said but that's ridiculous there's just not enough people to read everybody's correspondence, *D* said the computers read them and flags up keywords, like explosion, revolution, leak, freedom, accountability, any correspondence that raises enough flags are to be read by minions, and should you become of interest to somebody in the government, then there is a complete record of everything you've done electronically, Daisy's precious libertarian freedoms are being stomped in the face by government jackboots yes, but hay it's OK to be deeply offensive to others in that way now ain't it?

Emily said they couldn't store that much information not on everybody, *D* said digital voice calls are automatically transcribed into text files, any recorded conversation or comment, web searches, chat, post, everything goes into tiny little text files yes, Emily said OK it's insidious but it is necessary for everybody's safety, *D* sarcastically said yeah safety

Emily said if you have nothing to hide you have nothing to fear.

D said so you'd be OK with somebody setting up a government cams in your bedroom and toilet? If you have nothing to hide you have nothing to fear yes, or is privacy and freedom from constant intrusive surveillance important to you? Emily began to speak but then stopped herself, Daisy said cat got your tongue oppressor? Emily turned to look at Daisy sternly but remained silent.

D turning to James said, morality like with all evolutionary traits you're going to get variability's yes, so a sense of morality or a pattern of moral behaviour will vary between individuals, and as we ain't just individuals but an integral part of a social group, any sense of morality or a pattern of moral behaviour will also vary between social groups, and with all evolutionary traits it ain't just nature or nurture, it's the interplay between both simultaneously, that is the genetically inherited traits will influence behavioural responses, and behavioural responses will influence gene expression, this is an ongoing continues evolutionary process

James said huh?

D said OK people have lived for generations and generations in the northern hemisphere they developed light skin and blue eyes yes, James said well yes you adapt to the environment, *D* said that which was socially acceptable in the past ain't no longer considered socially acceptable today yes, James said well yes, *D* said so morality is adapting evolving yes, James said not for everybody some people have fixed philosophical or religious based morality, *D* said yes yes and horseshoe crabs still have blue blood they got hemocyanin not hemoglobin in their blood, there are evolutionary bottlenecks this happens yes, Catholicism evolved to symbolic sacrifices, where other religion's still sacrifice animals and people to their bloodthirsty gods, some groups are still living in primitive huts throwing stones at their own shadows to ward off the evil spirits of ignorance, while others are trying to colonise Mars, evolution does not happen in a uniform manner some become more evolved some less so

Emily was about to say something but stopped herself, *D* turned to Emily and said self-censorship? Emily tilted her head to one side and smiled sardonically.

D to James said morality is a functional response to the environment, it's a bunch of sometimes contradictory successful behaviour patterns, self-preservation verses group preservation with variation and occasional anomalies depending upon the environment and resources yes, because that's how evolution works, then slap on chemical inducements or emotions for good or bad behaviour like the capuchin monkey going apey, or you yourself feeling betrayed by George before you had a chance to reason yes, and when you had a chance to reason your template for good or bad behaviour "morality" is still adaptation survival propagation, or given these circumstances what is best for me and the group, or what threatens me and the group, and there you have it, any and I mean any moral decision you or anybody else make's will be rooted in DNA and evolutionary patterns yes, and any and all aspects of your or any other living evolving thing are necessarily bound to the same principles yes, so the function purpose or meaning of life is?

James thoughtfully rested his hand on his chin and said, you make a strong case, I will need to think about this.

D got up walked to the kitchen and made himself and *A* a coffee, people mingled about conversations began and the background noise level increased, after letting her coffee cool for a while *A* tasted her coffee spat it back in the cup then got up to make her own, sometime past and conversations ran out of steam and the background noise level decreased, and the low level background noise from behind a wall started to come into focus, feelings of anxiety and dark foreboding started to manifest amongst the group

Bertrice looked at Zandroe resting from his task of scoring the outline of a possible exit, the man was sweating despite having done precious little, Bertrice sternly said haven't you done that yet? Zandroe gave Bertrice a pitiful gaze as he said it's harder than it looks, Bertrice said just get on with it or let somebody else do it if you're incapable.

D said we're safe for now in here yes, and even if that is an exit which it may not be, we don't know what's waiting on the other side, Zandroe is doing fine, there is no rush to meet that unknown until we are all prepared yes, Bertrice gave a little huff and brushed some dust from her skirt, *D* smiled and winked at Zandroe

CHAPTER FREE, THERAVADA AND THE ART OF REDUCTION AD ABSURDUM

D turned towards Emily and said, earlier when I said less evolved you, stopped yourself from saying something what was that? Emily just smiled and said nothing *D* said you are the sum total of your memories experiences ideas and philosophies and feelings yes, so if somebody attack's your idea's or philosophy, you will consider it a personal attack upon yourself and you react accordingly, by getting all butt hurt yes, now if you have the wit to understand that if somebody criticizes or attack's an idea you have even if you hold that idea or philosophies dearly, it is not necessarily a personal attack upon yourself it is merely a criticism of that idea and nothing more yes, an idea like the earth is flat and is held up by five pillars is neither accurate nor useful in any way whatsoever, you can if you have the wit replace that bad idea with a better one, despite getting all butt hurt by reality yes

Emily sardonically smiling said I know the earth is round and I won't get all butt hurt by reality.

D said you were taught the earth is round at school or did you do the measurements yourself? Emily as if she was talking to a child said, at school, that's where you learn things (and then she emphasized the word.) yes, *D* said no that's where you're taught things, you are taught the earth is round but it ain't, in geometric terms it's an oblique spheroid, you were taught for convenience only, you were taught monkey see monkey do style, you were taught enough to operate the equipment, you were not taught how to think for yourself, if that would have happened well you might have become dangerous yes, now if you realise the difference between criticising an idea you hold, and a physical attack upon your person, and you're not going to get all butt hurt by reality, then we can have a sensible adult discussion yes, you stopped yourself from saying something when I said "less evolved" you think it sounds insulting demeaning?

Emily said yes *D* said but not inaccurate? Emily struggled thinking and then said I don't have the words, *D* said that's what censoring the language does, most people think in words, the more words you have the greater your ability to form an articulate idea's and vice versa yes. Censor the language, censor ideas, censor the ability to think critically, by basing the language ideas, entirely upon whether or not you might set off some crybullies artificial tears of victimhood, and not reality or the merit of the idea itself, Emily interjected if we change the language we can make the world a better place.

D laughed, Emily said don't you want to make the world a better place? *D* laughed more, Emily said so much for a sensible adult discussion, and then Emily folded her arms and looked sternly at *D*

D still chuckling said tyrannical censorship would make the world a better place?

Emily said no not tyrannical censorship just an adjustment in the language to make things less insulting less confrontational and friendlier.

D still chuckling said indeed we can ban the word starvation and replace it with the words rumbled tummies and then starvation will instantly disappear making the world a better place?

Emily said if you're not going to take this seriously, *D* said how can I it's delusional fluffy thinking spin, Emily said it's not delusional fluffy thinking spin, it's progressive it's the way forward, *D* said no, it's delusional fluffy thinking spin when you drop bombs murdering babies, then renaming it as collateral damage is not friendlier and more progressive, it does not make that something go-way like it never happen the babies are still very dead, you do realise this, you are vaguely aware of reality yes ? Emily said if we change our language then we can change our behaviour and that will change our reality, *D* said you would have to change the position of your eyes on your head for that to happen, Emily said huh?

D said the eyes at the front of your head are there so you can judge the distance to your prey, human beings are predator's, although amongst the slowest apex predator's, we are unrivalled long distance land endurance hunters, we run our prey down to exhaustion, we are determined relentless ruthless meat eating killers, and no amount of delusional spin will change that, Emily said I'm a vegetarian I don't run around killing anything, we can change we can evolve, we can progress, *D* said we certainly can we are one of the most adaptable species on the planet, and with a constant supply of food we become passive docile fat, although we are always, always only three meals a way from anarchy, and two weeks away from cannibalism, our very nature will not be changed by a wave of the delusional political correct social injustice warriors wand, and when a world changing disaster happens, as it has happened in the past and is happening now, and as it will happen in the future, it was never an if, it's always a when, then you'll need that fight or flight response, you will need that savage aggression which defines us as a species, hypothetically if your adopted idea had actually changed our reality to some hugs and bunnies and everybody being nice passive and docile permanently utopia, then we'd just die as a species at the first worldwide disaster yes.

D shook his head and then said I know that when certain groups become isolated and detached from reality, and they get high sniffing their own bullshit in the twisted echo chamber of their corrupted minds, they become self-destructive and genocidal, as subconsciously they realise their own pathetic irrelevance in the scheme of things, as they watch everything they touched ultimately turning to shit, pahh dumbasses eugenicists, *D* raised his hands in mock surrender while saying my apologies I do tend to rant while performing reductio ad absurdum.

Emily said I am not detached from reality nor am I sniffing my own bullshit, and the world is unsustainably overpopulated, *D* said and how would you know this? Emily look confused and then said know what? *D* said either i-ther both, how do you know you are not detached, and how do you know the world is unsustainably overpopulated?

Emily said just open your eyes and you'll see the world is unsustainably overpopulated, *D* said now? Pointing towards the door with his e-cigarette, Emily said no not now obviously but before.

D said just open your eyes and you'll see the world looks as flat as a pancake, back in the eighteen hundreds there was that Zetetic astronomy five hundred pounds sterling competition to the person who could prove the world was round, because the world was so obviously flat at the time, the Bedford level experiment yes, looks can be very deceiving yes, people rooted in reality tend to realise this and usually avoid saying, just open your eyes or it's obvious, as reality is often counter intuitive yes, do you have something more substantial to support this theory Emily?

Emily with a tad of frustration said it's obvious the world is... Was unsustainably overpopulated why can't you see this?

D said unsustainably overpopulated is a catchphrase it's a hook the kind of thing television advertising companies absolutely drool over, and your television has been repeating the word overpopulated to you ad nauseam before you could even talk, the repeated phrase will cause synaptic connections to be made and reinforced so you end up thinking, literally thinking the ideas connected with the repeated phrase are your own, it's subtle insidious brainwashing, you end up believing something is absolutely true based upon no hard cold evidence whatsoever, the very definition of delusional yes.

Emily said I'm not delusional and I know I'm right, just try to prove it otherwise.

D said ho the shifting burden of proof, just try to prove father Christmas or the tooth fairy doesn't exist yes, searching your mind for evidence to back up your claim, you came up empty yes, and the seeds of doubt have been planted, how should we nurture these seeds some history perhaps, were there any previous claims of overpopulation with limited resources, and inescapable doom, and the end is nigh! *D* raised his hands above his head shaking his wrists for mock dramatic effect, then he lowered his arms and continued to say, that just didn't pan out, because the theory was utterly flawed in some way yes?

Emily said I don't know I'm not a historian, and just because it wasn't true then, that doesn't mean it's not true now ...I mean then... you're confusing me, *D* smiling said I bet the civil service just loved you, I'll try to keep this as simple as possible, Emily said why thank you for implying I'm an idiot, then she said tilting her head to one side where you one of them? You talk like them kind-of, *D* said no, and I'm not implying that you're an idiot, you're just misinformed and ignorant, Emily sardonically said why that's far less insulting and condescending, *D* said ignorance is simply a state of not knowing, we are both ignorant of many things yes ? Emily said well yes I suppose, *D* said you believe without knowing any substantiated facts that the world was overpopulated yes, Emily said like I said prove me wrong, *D* said an enlightened person would question their own assumptions, an intelligent person asks others.

Ellicott to *D* said so hang on you said earlier that television is brainwashing are you some kind of conspiracy theorist? Do you think the lizard people are trying to control us?

D said conspiracy theorist oh my yes "et tu, brute" or in English you too Brutus, supposedly the last words of Julius Caesar, supposedly a group of senators conspired to kill Caesar thus conspiracy, an act of conspiring "a combination of persons for an evil or unlawful purpose" although there is no direct physical evidence of the act of the assassination of Julius Caesar, it's all just rumor and hearsay so one must speculate theorise yes, so like all students of history I certainly do engage in conspiracy theories, about this supposed act of assassination and other's yes, history itself is resplendent with conspiracies yes, the Borgia, the knights' Templar, Rasputin, everybody loves a good conspiracy, it's part of our very language "Friday the thirteenth" "the saint valentine's day massacre" "beware the ides of march" as for lizard people trying to control us, most unlikely I think, although social engineers I believe they are trying to control us, the clue is in a job title yes.

Ellicott said so you think social engineers are controlling us through television, then Ellicott gave a dismissive huff.

D said social engineering is a branch of psychology, and advertising companies have been employing psychologists for years, perhaps you should have told them not to waste their time or the trillions upon trillions they spent in trying to control your behaviour through advertising yes

Ellicott said well it didn't work on me.

D said really so you have absolutely no branded products in your home? Or was the control so subtle you didn't even notice it happening yes? Ellicott said nothing, *D* said and that's just a tiny slice of your scheduled programming time, seconds in the hours, of your passive willing acceptance of the sleek and shiny dissinfotainment yes, do you honestly believe that what you watched was neither biased nor agenda driven in any way whatsoever?

Ellicott said that's all just nonsense, I suppose you believe the first moon landings in nineteen sixty-nine never happened.

D said I don't know I wasn't on the moon to witness it myself

Henry said now come on there's evidence for those first moon landings, the moon rocks which I've seen myself, the rockets which I've seen myself, all the people that worked on the project, even the Russian's believed it they monitored the conversations tracked the spacecraft and printed it in their newspaper, the evidence is overwhelming

D said then there should be no controversy but there is, ain't there?

Henry said tinfoil hat wearing conspiracy nut jobs that believe in Bigfoot the Loch Ness monster, and the earth is flat.

D said why certainly you have your tinfoil hat wearing nut jobs, yet you also have many conspiracy theorists that have been proven correct yes, like your government is in fact spying on you, or the world's best cyclists were on steroids, or "the fruit machine" a nineteen sixties secret north American government gay detector, three cherries and your outed, although I think it was actually based upon eye dilation, the list of at first denied and called crazy conspiracy theories, that in time were admitted to be true is very long and sometimes extremely bizarre and very sinister yes, conspiracies happen people politicians governments and government organizations work in secret and lie, even scientists lie Henry, if a government sponsored scientist said that the sky was blue, I'd need to check that for myself, such cynicism is warranted based upon the sheer amount of historical government spin and outright bullshit yes, between the tinfoil hat wearing conspiracy nut jobs and the official government spokesman I'd choose to believe neither, unless the evidence supports the claim

Henry said but it does I've seen it with my own eyes, I am certain that the first moon landings happened the evidence is overwhelming.

D said all the evil done in this world is done by people that are certain

Henry said what?

D said it's an old Buddhist saying, then *D* said the evidence the moon rocks yes, the Russian's brought back some moon rocks with a probe in the nineteen sixties, do the Russian moon rocks prove cosmonauts landed on the moon in the nineteen sixties? They had a rocket big enough to stick a probe on the moon dose this prove cosmonauts landed on the moon? The Americans tracked the Russian spaceship, and the returning probe does this prove cosmonauts landed on the moon? If the Russian's had stuck a timed pre-recorded playback machine so they could have faked a two way conversation, would that count as proof?

Henry said NASA doesn't fake

D said well apart from the moon rock given to Holland by Neil Armstrong and Buzz Aldrin that turned out to be a fake, governments and government organizations lie it's what they do, is the evidence overwhelming? Lots of questionable or contested evidence does not equate to undeniable overwhelming proof, could it have been faked ... yes, so I neither believe the tinfoil hat wearing conspiracy nut jobs or the official spokesman, I'd like to think we did, but as it is still controversial and mired in claim and counter-claim, did we land on the moon in the nineteen sixties? I don't know I wasn't on the moon to witness it myself.

Henry said but why would they fake it?

D said it was the space race and America was suffering morale sapping humiliating defeat after humiliating defeat, first satellite in space Russia, first animal in space Russia first man in space Russia first woman in space Russia first spacewalk Russia, and so on, and this was during the cold war and "all warfare is based upon deception" Sun Tzu the art of war "or if at first you don't succeed, cheat, repeat until caught, and then lie!" it's the real motto of every government, and it's organizations on the planet yes, motive means and opportunity it was all there.

Henry said and the witnesses? And the people who worked on the project?

D said how many of those people that worked on the project were actually on the moon to see them step out? And how many witnesses have seen the Loch Ness monster including bona fide upstanding professional pillars of the community and all?

Henry said I still believe, despite what you've said, and I think it was too big to fake.

D smiling said, well good for you but do you understand my position?

Henry said well I suppose if you're a very cynical sceptic.

D said ain't that the basis of scientific methodology?

Henry raised his eyebrows and then nodded then he said did Armstrong and Buzz really give Holland a fake rock? *D* said they really did, Henry said it could have just been a mistake, *D* said could have

D turned to Ellicott and said anymore self-evidently well practised ad-hominess's or strawmen? Ellicott pretended not to hear.

D turned to Emily and said now where were we before we were rudely interrupted? oh yes, me "you believe without knowing any substantiated facts that the world was overpopulated yes" you "like I said prove me wrong"

Emily said how do you do that, remember conversations exactly?

D said as I said earlier, I can only remember conversations verbatim for five or so years, it gets a bit fuzzy after that, I've got an acoustic memory I remember the words to songs I don't even like and have only heard just the once, and it still surprises me when somebody tries to sing along but only managers to blurt out the chorus to a song they had been listening to repeatedly for decades, how can they not remember every single word, every single pause every inflection, every vocal stumble?

Emily said I'm a blurter I just don't really listen to the words intently, but I do try to sing along occasionally, embarrassingly usually when inebriated she laughed with the soft giggle, then Emily said you said acoustic memory?

D said it's just genetic variability for some it's audio others visual for some smell or touch or even situation, some have a terrible memory while others have a photographic memory, all can be advantageous under the right circumstances, so what's yours?

Emily said a terrible memory I think she giggled then said perhaps numbers I'm good at remembering registration plates passwords birthdays anniversaries appointments, numbers I think, not photographic but I have a good memory for numbers, but you said there not real, numbers I mean, *D* said yes abstract imaginary extremely useful but not a true reflection of how the universe works, Emily said that doesn't sit right in my head, somehow I'm not sure I can explain it I don't have the words, and I'm normally good with words, not remembering conversations exactly, but I'm good at talking and using words, and this isn't coming out right, I can't explain myself and that's frustrating, I think it maybe you somehow I'm not normally like this

D said thinking is hard work, it burns a lot of calories, and burning calories while you're fighting for survival can be deadly, evolution favours the conservation of energy, yet at the same time, out thinking you're prey can be the key to survival, an interesting contradiction yes, there are tricks shortcuts if you will in thinking that can conserve those precious life sustaining calories, like let somebody else do the thinking and just follow them, as a politician you must be well aware of this, follow the blue philosophy or follow the red philosophy a calorie saving binary choice, a tribalistic herd mentality choice, and belonging to a group is comforting yes, us good them bad, most of the world's population believe that the universe itself works on mathematics, so when I say it don't, and then show why it don't, that herd mentality kicks in and you feel you should reject this idea that goes against the flow, although you can't think why exactly except "them bad" somehow, does this explain your position and frustration?

Zandroe laughed and said I've never seen the like, why aren't you running the world? *D* smiling sheepishly said who says I'm not? Zandroe said "itinerant worker" you should be the richest man in the world in some hollowed out volcano or something, *D* just laughed, Zandroe again said I've never seen the like, then he returned to scoring the wall.

Emily said so basically you're saying I'm an idiot again? *D* said like I said thinking is hard work and burns a lot of calories, so we all tend to take the shortcuts that evolution has provided, Emily said except you, *D* said no not exactly, even though I'm perhaps aware of some of my own cognitive bias and cognitive dissidence and so on, it is a hard fight to overcome these, and it is a fight I usually lose, the seduction of the easy expected accepted answer is always there yes, while doubt and uncertainty and the idea of fruitless pursuit are always ever present clawing at my very reason whispering give up do something else, do nothing, Emily said so you don't know it all then? *D* said nope, I have perhaps a few of the fundamentals not much more

Henry to *D* said so you didn't manage to solve the grand unification problem then?

D said oh Einstein's unfinished theory, the theory of everything, yep I solved that, Henry barked what! No come on, *D* said yer that wasn't a particularly difficult one, Henry said I'm caught between disbelief and adulation here, you solved it and didn't bother telling anybody? *D* said well everybody seem to be having so much fun on the journey of discovery I didn't want to spoil it for them, Henry said what no! The grand unification theory solved, and you didn't want to spoil the fun by telling anybody, I cannot believe what I'm hearing.

Zandroe said what is the grand unification theory? *D* waving his hands in the air for dramatic effect said the theory of everything, it's the problem Einstein was working on before he died, Einstein's last great unfinished theory, it's like this you've got classical Newtonian physics the motions of the planet's and so on, and you've got quantum physics or quantum mechanics the motion of particles and so on, both predictive mathematical models but they don't play nice together, in the cold unforgiving light of reality, so you need something to marry the two mathematical models together, thus the grand unification theory the, theory of everything *D* waved his hands in the air for dramatic effect again, Zandroe said OK, and you can marry the two together?

D said nope I worked out I couldn't do it, I also worked out nobody else could do it either, Zandroe said that's not exactly solved is it? *D* said, when you prove something is unprovable ain't that a proof? Zandroe said I don't know?

CHAPTER THOR THE THEORY OF EVERYTHING

Henry to *D* said go on then let's have it

D said I've already done it, it's already there, laid right out in front of you yes, when I asked why does one plus one equal two, with the answer of we've made it up, and that mathematics is an abstract concept that ain't no true reflection of how the universe works, or that the universe itself does not work on monkey grunts yes, and that the universe itself does not work on the law of identity or of excluded middle logic, which you yourself confirmed was empirically proven, with quantum superposition that is one particle being in multiple places simultaneously, it's all right there, Isaac Newton invented classical physics which was wonderful it ushered in the new age of discovery for mankind, as the idea of a clockwork universe was born, and the clockwork universe was believed so absolutely some of the greatest minds on the planet set about creating Principia Mathematica, a book setting out the very foundations of mathematics for this clockwork universe that would quantify and explain everything, Kurt Gödel put a spanner in the works questioning achievable levels of complexity, and Principia Mathematica should have been abandoned, although you didn't need Kurt Gödel to point out Principia Mathematica was fundamentally flawed, as the entire enterprise was to me at least self-evidently just an exercise in fluffy thinking from the start yes, Principia Mathematica a grand piece of theatre and the mighty tomb, that “proves” one plus one equals two, using symbolic logic to prove symbols like 1 and 2 have symbolic meanings, gotta love it, using symbolic logic to prove symbolic logic, a magnificent piece of circular reasoning worthy of Descartes himself

D continue to say anyhow’s the clockwork universe model was and is still usable and still incredibly useful so let's ignore Kurt, describe his work as an interesting but irrelevant quirk, ignore the self-evident circular reasoning, and carry on regardless, anyhow’s during the time of Principia Mathematica, quantum physics was starting to step into its own, and a new age of discovery for mankind began thanks to Einstein who updated Isaac Newton's clockwork universe model, although Einstein himself was not overly happy with his own results, he liked the clockwork universe model, not the messy quantum physics model, Einstein imagined a universe created as if he had made it himself, ordered sensible reasonable understandable, as Einstein said “God does not play dice with the universe” but the quantum physics model turned out to be probabilistic which ain't neat and tidy yes, and here’s the thing Einstein knew Kurt Gödel personally, he should have realized that God ain’t using monkey grunts to determine the behaviour of the universe

D looked to Junia and said Einstein was using the word God metaphorically as am I, then *D* continued to say, anyhow’s Einstein’s updated clockwork universe mathematical model was wonderful it ushered in the new age of discovery and gave us the world's most famous mathematical equation $E\wedge^{2}=(MC^{2})\wedge^{2}+(PC)\wedge^{2}$, or $E=MC^{2}$ all very neat and tidy yes, or it can be described as equivalents energy equals mass, or you can do away with the mathematics and equivalents altogether and just say energy is all, there is no mass, just energy fields

D looked at the floor and said the thing stopping you from falling to the centre of the earth is the electromagnetic energy fields bonding particles together, although the word particles is unnecessary as there is no real substance to them it's all just energy and I ... we've used too many words to describe one and the same thing, E is and there ain't no-more to it than that yes, as a species we do tend to pontificate too much, anyhow's I'm pontificating too much, where was I ? oh yes Newton Einstein you me were all enthralled with mathematics, we use it every day and it works demonstrably, and the higher level mathematics becomes beautiful poetry or music, and it all works demonstrably, well no it don't, a mathematical proof needs to be confirmed empirically, because the maths can prove almost anything, and there's the rub, Newton's mathematical model worked well enough-ish, where many others didn't and were forgotten, Einstein's model worked better-ish, where many others didn't and were forgotten, can you see a pattern forming here ? Lots of mathematical models, the more successful ones fitted the empirical observations.

Henry said, but Einstein's mathematical theories predicted black holes long before they were ever observed empirically, mathematics is predictive which shows the truth of it.

D said Einstein's mathematical theories, predicted a singularity at the centre of a black hole, infinite density. oh my an infinite, infinite's can exist in mathematics, but not in the real universe, if a black-hole singularity was infinitely dense then it would have an infinite gravitational pull, and it would swallow up the entire universe yes.

Eva said I thought the universe was infinite

D said nope this universe has a beginning, to be infinite it would require an infinite amount of time, which it just ain't got, you can work out the size of the universe approximately using the beginning time and the speed of light, the start was about fourteen billion years ago giving the universe a size of about twenty-eight billion light years across, although this is very speculative if at the boundaries the temperature is absolute zero that is minus two seven three point one five degrees Celsius then matter-energy starts behaving very strangely at those temperatures, but the universe may not be expanding into nothingness at absolute zero, it could be expanding into a vacuum, like a previous failed or almost dead universe, or it could be expanding into a multiverse, this would explain a-lot, but well who knows ?

Eva smiling said I'm surprised you don't, *D* smiling said I'm working on it I have an inkling but I'd need time to work on it

Henry said but still Einstein's theories work, *D* said a-lot of his theories do-ish yes, and numerous theories put forward by others didn't, first there was the theory, then there was the mathematics, then there was the empirical confirmation, magnificent old school science in action, that opened the door to quantum physics or quantum mechanics I'm old school so I say physics, as I've yet to see a quantum mechanic in dirty oil covered overalls with a spanner in hand, old school physics old school science, new school science is usually accidentally discovered empirical, with shoehorned post hoc mathematics, and then some kind of theory bolted on, if mathematics truly described the universe then we would know gravity from the universal down to the quantum scale yes, but we don't, we don't even know how a transistor actually works.

John Runndolf the chemist interjected we know how transistor's actually work we've been using them for decades, computer chips are transistor based, even I know that

D said know how to use them yes, know how they actually work no, oh there are many great and mighty authoritative people and institutions that can describe band's and electron holes and quasiparticle's, and incalculable scholarly articles and papers describing semiconductors in solid state physics in pedantic detail, but it's just the least laughable and most usable approximations, trying to describe the thus far incomprehensible observable empirical reality yes, nobody really knows, *D* smiled then said thus far, anyhow's we have working approximations that are good enough, to put a satellite in and around our own solar system, and to build the electronics needed to achieve that, which is remarkable, although in galactic terms that's still inside the baby's crib for a species, but to put a satellite in orbit around our neighbour Star bob's dwarf ? That's just outside the baby's crib no... no, the working approximations just ain't good enough for that; the language of the universe is hopefully discoverable, but it sure ain't monkey grunts mathematics therefore you cannot unite mathematics with reality, despite having a pretty good mostly working approximation, if you don't scale it up too big or small or take it too far forward or backwards in time yes.

A said the *D*-imperative, conscious perceptual framing limitations, then she rolled her eyes, *D* to *A* said you yourself coined that phrase yes. *A* said yes when your ugly reality tarnished the beauty and art of my mathematics and geometry. *D* said I merely pointed out its fundamental flaws and thus its limitations, it still useful and usable it's just limited in its practical application, and calling it "my" and subscribing attributes like art and beauty anthropomorphizing it, highlights that tarnish yes. *A* said you'll never understand, *D* said I understand letting go is hard. *A* huffed rolled her eyes but said nothing

Henry said but you need mathematics to understand quantum physics, *D* to Henry said do you understand quantum physics? Henry pulled a face shrugged his shoulders and shook his head.

D said mathematics opened the door to quantum physics but it cannot fully step through it, Henry said that's depressing, *D* said it's liberating there is a language to be discovered yes, and it's probably staring us right in the face, simple elegant and so obvious everybody will wonder why nobody spotted it, just like matter is energy yes, Henry said so have you worked out that language? *D* smiling said not yet I'm still working on it, I have perhaps some vague notions, but to go forward I need a reliable indication of how the speed of light is fluctuating yes.

Henry said the speed of light C is thee universal constant, I've heard of some wild proposals by some on the fringe to make it a variable but I can't see that going anywhere.

D said it's the mathematics if C became a variable, it throws all the mathematics out of kilter, and that would be chaos, for physics and atomic dating yes.

Henry said well yes without that fixed point modelling and progress would come to a standstill, you'd have to recalculate everything every time C changed including $E=MC^2$ it's just unthinkable.

D said Einstein tried updating C with a variable speed of light proposal back in the early nineteen hundreds, but it was messy, and not adopted, but that's because he was using the wrong mathematical language yes, like I said we need a new mathematical language

Henry said I never knew Einstein tried updating C as a variable, and a new mathematical language, I don't think that has ever been done before, not in the entire history of mankind, all mathematical systems are based on numbers, where would you even start trying to think up a usable alternative?

D said ho the starting bit is easy, and the Chinese invented an alternative mathematical system using music, a tuned hand bell for a rice scoop, everybody could hear if you were cheating on the portions, and a tuned guitar string for length, I'd like a suit in a *D#* major chord fit please, Henry and *D* laughed as *D* pulled on his lapels, Henry said so music would be the starting point? *D* said that ain't the starting point I was thinking of, but it certainly is a possibility yes, good thinking Henry could you expand on that idea? Henry thoughtfully said well now .... Then Henry said let me think for a sec, if you .... As *D* and Henry conversed.

CHAPTER PENTAGON, THE VERY DEVIL HIMSELF

John, the desk clerk said to Karl and Junia I was almost following that conversation between that know it all gorilla and the physicist but now they're just talking gibberish.

Junia said I don't trust him he's shifty and manipulative, and he's too clever and too arrogant, there's something not quite right about him, and why does he call himself *D*?

Karl said it's you know just a tag like init, but he's certain got's being an old bad boy arted

Junia said tag? Karl said tag you know it's like a nickname init, like avatar online handle like, Junia said why would he use an online nickname in real life?

John the desk clerk said I don't know J perhaps as a child you have a given name, and as an adult you give yourself a chosen name, Junia said don't start acting like him, all smug arrogant and condescending it doesn't suit you, John the desk clerk said but it does suit him somehow despite his look's, he's got a bunch of high end academics looking like ignorant children, is that arrogance or confidence? Karl said init and that *A* what's her story like? Karl looked at *A*, *A* somehow noticed and glared back at him, Karl looked away sharply, Junia said I've never seen you shy before Karl.

Karl said so like what's our escape plan? John the desk clerk said I'm with Junia whatever happens, Karl said yer yer the secret love affair that everybody cotton to init, Junia face was turning red, Junia turned away as John the desk clerk said everybody knew? Karl smiling said serious like everybody init, but I don't fink's that's ure worry's nar bra, the escape plan like?

John the desk clerk said there looks like two exits, the window and that secret passage, if that's what it is, and it goes anywhere, Junia said I don't like the idea of a tunnel, Karl said I don't like the idea of zombies or burning to death like, but it is what it is init

John, the desk clerk, said then its Hobson's choice, Junia said what? John the desk clerk said take it or leave it, that's what Hobson's choice mean's, the window or nothing, Junia said I didn't say I wouldn't use the tunnel, I just said I didn't like the idea of it, I don't like the idea of heights or falling out of the window either.

Karl facepalmed and shook his head with his face covered by his palm, Junia said I'm frightened and I don't know what to think or do, then she started sobbing, John the desk clerk started comforting her while saying don't worry I won't leave you no matter what, Karl had an epiphany looked up and said victims.

John the desk clerk shot Karl a fierce narrow eyed gaze, Karl just looked back at John the desk clerk and said unless one of you grows a pair quick like, ure just victims, you realise that don't you, Junia started sobbing harder, and John the desk clerk's attention was drawn back to her.

Karl was calm and relaxed and yet somehow not, his epiphany was starting to fade but for a moment it was all so crystal clear all laid right out in front of him, as if he was just recalling some past event of his own life with dramatic clarity, they would both die here huddled together, Junia paralysed by fear and John paralysed by empathetic fear for his love.

Karl's mind raced searching for solutions for a way out of this ridiculous situation, scenarios presented themselves but they were then rejected and replaced by new futile scenarios, the calm and relaxed state he was in earlier was ebbing away like the last of the water down the bath plug replaced by anxiety replaced by fear.

Karl stopped himself, fear it will lead Junia and John to paralysing hopeless apathy and death init, Karl didn't want this, these were his friends, but he didn't want to get dragged down into the hopeless spiral himself, perhaps he was wrong, perhaps this was only a fleeting schism and they would all leave together, but then what he pondered ? Then what? He had seen for himself the chaos outside, and the fires and the smoke, the smoke *D* had said that would help to camouflaged them init, when it became thick enough like, he knew the area well enough, he just had to wait for an opportune moment, then out the window init, he had figured the familiar surroundings would be better than some unfamiliar secret passage if that was what it was like, but what if that passage led to safety? No, the familiar was his best bet like, the familiar the family who had said that earlier like? He looked at Junia sat on the floor legs drawn in close, and her arms wrapped around her legs in the seated foetal position rocking backwards and forwards slowly, red eyes sobbing quietly to herself now, John trying desperately to comfort her.

Karl snapped his train of thought back, what then, what then? The familiar the family my family, the woman that sacrificed herself in so many ways to raise me like, and now she's in a nursing home in Devon hundreds of miles away like, I got'ta to contact that nursing home like to tell them to warn them init, to tell them to keep my grandmother safe until I get there like, it's my responsibility init, I need to think like, I need to work this out while I have time to think like, the trains won't be running, the car's won't work in this chaos like they stop for hedgehogs and frogs init, frogs there was a two hour delay for frogs one time when I went to visit my grandmother during the summer like.

Karl remembered the annoying repeated sympathetic voice coming out of the car's loudspeakers interrupting his music and any chance of a relaxing snooze “important environmental work in progress no alternative routes available” the ecomentalist' let car's through one at a time causing a huge tailback like, oh them ecomentalist came to apologise like along the long line of car’s, while trying to guilt trip there captive audience for money and membership to the glorious cause like, they was jamed about my extended middle finger in response, I’s sure I weren't the only donator of a middle finger that day like, I really should’er taken that car stop wand gizmo and fat shamed it right up that ecomentalist arss like, and then played happy frog stomp, I's sure them other frustrated ecomentalist vic's would have joined in like given the spur like, no stop ... my mind is wandering I need a plan and the clock is ticking init, so how to get to Devon to my grandmother like? Perhaps there's an old style manual car somewhere, or a motorbike that was it a motorbike init, the electricity is still on, I can still get a charge like and Devon is only a couple of hundred miles away, and there's a bike blagroom not two miles away init, I bet’s Mr smarty pants over there h’an't gleaned of this like, I'll wait until he stops yakking with that prof or whatever like then I'll tell him init.

Karl noticed John and Junia had calmed down which was comforting, then he listened in to *D*’s and Henry’s conversation, waiting for his opportunity

D said to Henry you are still thinking of discrete packets of energy, try to think of it as the single energy field merging with itself, Henry said but that makes no sense, *D* said OK try to think of it as an enormous river with tiny little whirlpools, if the circumstances are right these tiny little whirlpools merge and increase in their energy gravitational potential if the circumstances are not right they bounce off each other, but it's all in the same larger energy gravitational potential, the same river yes, Henry said but this goes against the way I think and its tough meat to chew, James said sorry to interrupt but this has been nagging me, if the universe and everything in it is just one big energy field or whatever, what about identity ? *D* said the identity problem to James, and then said the observer problem to Henry, *D* refilled his e-pipe then inhaled deeply and let out a cloud of steam, Bertrice let out some fake coughs and waved her hand in front of her face, *D* chuckled then said to James and Henry consciousness, as Karl simultaneously a little too loudly blurted out the word motorbikes, they were both silent for a moment then *D* smiling said Zen consciousness and motorbikes?

Karl looked confused for a second, then a little too quickly he said like there's a motorbike blagroom not two miles away init, then he pointed and continue to say that way like

D asked just new bikes? And does it have its own garage? Karl said new and old and it has a garage and a MOT like, *D* said excellent information thank you Karl, as people in the group started conversing with each other about motorbikes, Karl questioningly said well? *D* said the situation outside makes all but the most generalised plans apt to failure, personally I'll be heading for the river, as I consider that to be the safest mode of transport, Karl said boats I h'an't thought of that like.

D said where are you heading for Karl? Karl said my grandmother init she's in Devon on the south coast like, *D* said I lived in the north side for a while, beautiful isolated, and at this time of year not many people there, if you can get yourself and your grandmother high enough, in an old mine or cave that should afford you some protection against what is to come yes, Karl said like that Sun thing you was yakking about is that for serious like? *D* said yep its periodic mankind has been through this before and has lived and survived in caves before, early man didn't move deep into caves for the scenic view's you know, you should be relatively safe from the Sun at least at night, and you should have some innate awareness or some subtle feeling when it isn't safe, trust those feelings, as the Sun isn't the only sky monster emitting high energy particles out there yes, anyhow's a motorbike is not an unreasonable mode of transport given the circumstances, but I'd swap it for a tractor or industrial vehicle at the earliest opportunity, if I was going overland.

John the chemist said there is an airport not too far from here, and I have a pilot's licence, *D* said air travel could be problematic I think, under these circumstances England may have been turned into a no fly zone to try to contain the infection, drones missiles lasers all kinds of unpleasantness could well be on auto fire by now I think yes, John the chemist said I didn't think of that, and then John the chemist said if there is a military quarantine zone wouldn't that include boats ? *D* said most likely yes, I don't plan to cross the English Channel in a boat, for that very reason, I'm thinking about taking a boat to the south coast and then I'd use the channel tunnel if feasible

D said so where are you off to John? John, the chemist said couldn't this infection? (He pointed towards the door with the infected behind it) Couldn't it be confined to England? And couldn't you be unwittingly spreading it if you went abroad?

D said yes that is entirely possible, although I consider it most unlikely yes, John the chemist said why? *D* said I believe it would be reasonable to assume that the infection is a torus spreading outwards, *A* and I were... As to say herded away from its centre I think, John the chemist said where were you when err you know? And he waved an arm towards the door with the infected behind it again, *D* said between Heathrow and the rugby ground, John the chemist said Twickenham

D nodded, John the chemist then said there was a big match on earlier today, *D* said yep but that weren't the direction we were being herded away from, John the chemist said the world's busiest airport, *D* said yep the world's busiest airport, John the chemist said arr yes I see what you mean if it didn't come in by plane than its most likely gone out by plane *D* said the Americas might be OK assuming that the Americas weren't ground zero, John the chemist said yes the crossing time is hours, but to France Belgium or Amsterdam it's minutes

D said so where were you thinking of going John? John the chemist said just up up and away, find out what's happening on the old squawk box, and then take it from there, not much of a plan I know but it felt right somehow you-know, *D* said time for a new plan I think yes, John the chemist slowly and thoughtfully while scratching his chin said yes, then he said why don't I tag along with you two? If that's OK, I mean.

D said are you OK with some company *A*? *A* shrugged her shoulders and then said will it make any difference? *D* said you're coming off an adrenalin high, and things are looking bleak but ... *A* interrupted bleak? What is this word bleak?

Eva said morne sombre, the word bleak I think is old English northern possibly derived from the Norse, but don't quote me on that.

A said sombre oui very fucking bleak, *D* said we're alive with danger excitement and adventure stretching out before us, and if we die then we have no more worries yes.

A said and if we turn into those things? *D* said that's an unknown and unknowns are scary "the undiscovered country from whose bourn no traveller returns, that puzzles the will and makes us rather bear those ills we have, than fly to others that we know not of, thus conscience does make cowards of us all" or the unknown scares the crap out of everybody yes

Eva said Shakespeare hamlet to be or not to be again, I'm thinking... not to be, I'm old tired and slow, and I need a handful of pills everyday just to keep going, she pulled some silver foil covered pills and some pills in a small plastic bottle out of her tweed jacket pocket, then she said and these just in case, that undiscovered country doesn't look so scary to me, I think I'll just stay here when the rest of you leave, I think that's probably for the best.

D said Eva could any of those pills be useful to those that leave, painkillers stimulants? Junia said with the harsh tone to her voice you are the very devil himself, *D* looked at *A* and *A* looked at *D* they smiled and they said simultaneously seventy two, *D* looked at Junia and said the number of times I've been called the very devil himself in the presence of *A* she's a mathematician she likes to count these type of things

Zandroe said that's quite insensitive *D*, Eva is a human being you know, she deserves some respect. *D* said do you show respect by bullshitting, should I treat her like a child and say everything is going to be Ok when it blatantly won't, out of respect? Zandroe raised an eyebrow and looked uncomfortable

D continued to say, social politeness does have its place, it's the bullshit we tell each other to form a tolerable society, no your hair looks nice, or they're coming up with new cures all the time I'm sure your be fine, I consider Eva to be an intelligent individual, so out of respect I'm treating her as such, and not some uber sensitive adult with delicate sensibilities and a self retarded child's mind

Zandroe said but it still doesn't feel right, *D* said that's social conformity speaking, the same social conformity that gives you a guilt free made by child slave labour shiny new mobile phone yes, Zandroe reached for the outside of his inside jacket pocket feeling the device, Zandroe said but everybody has one.

D looked at Junia and said no not everybody, the very devil himself tries hard not to patronise evil financially. Junia instinctively reached for her phone in her jeans then looked away.

Zandroe said so *D* you're the most moral person in the world; it must be irksome for you to mingle with us lesser mortals. *D* smiling said yes, but not for moral reasons, Zandroe's mouth fell open.

D said I defined morality remember, but I ain't no divine Buddha like practitioner of it, pointing out your moral hypocrisy and inadequacies does not lessen mine in any way whatsoever, although it does bring me a certain sense of smug satisfaction in doing so, Zandroe rolled his eyes, *D* continued to say, let's look at the situation for what it is yes, and try to discard all the well-practised and rehearsed apocryphal social virtue signalling bullshit, Eva has made her decision let us all respect that decision, and see what we can do to help the others yes, Zandroe said with your intellect you could probably argue black is white, Ellicott snorted then said impossible. Zandroe continued to say but it doesn't make what you've said right *D*

Eva said, I just said what I said to try to elicit some help, I don't want you to respect my decision I want you to talk me out of it, and then help me out of here.

A laughed and looked at *D* and said you didn't see that one did you? *D* said cognitive biases I was hoping for the Grace sacrifice so we didn't have to deal, and then there was the potential benefit of stim's and painkillers, Junia said the very devil himself, *D* looked at *A* and *A* looked at *D* they smiled and they said simultaneously seventy three.

Zandroe said I bet you're not feeling so smug now are you *D*? *A* said give him a few moments and his intolerable chirpy smugness shall return, Zandroe said to *A* how do you stand it? *A* said that intellect is disturbing revealing frightening and intoxicating and normally he's quiet, while I'm the chatty one, be careful what you ask him and be careful about what you say to him, that intellect of his can be ruthless.

Zandroe said so I'd gathered but it's not flawless, *A* said just like everybody else he hears what he wants to hear and sees what he wants to see, that intellect of his cuts through a lot of bullshit, but not all of it, and if you manage to point out a flaw in his reasoning he will be truly grateful, where I still struggle with criticism. Zandroe said as do we all I think, *D* said smugly there are always exceptions, oh said *A* his smugness is back, did you figure out a way of saving Eva? *D* said nope I just figured that those that are fit willing and able enough should go through the window, *D* looked over to Junia and John the desk clerk and said and the newlyweds and the nearly dead's should go through the trapdoor, Eva being Zandroe's responsibility yes.

Zandroe said my responsibility? I'm not exactly the responsible type, *D* said but you argued so eloquently on her behalf yes, Zandroe said but if this isn't a door, and even if it is and it goes nowhere? *D* said I'm sure everything is going to be OK, Zandroe said isn't that the polite social bullshit you were talking about earlier? *D* smiling said you can call it political correctness if you'd like, then he turned to Eva and in a mocking sarcastic tone said don't do it Eva, think of all those grammatically incorrect people that you can save from themselves, and Zandroe is willing to risk life and limb to save you, there you go Eva.

Eva dryly said thank you while eyeing Zandroe suspiciously, then while momentarily looking at *D* she continued to say I think Junia may have been right about you, *A* looked at *D* and *D* looked at *A* they shrugged simultaneously, *D* then said I suppose sharing those med's around is completely out of the question, Eva with a sardonic smile repeated, completely out of the question, Zandroe was about to say something to *D* as *D* turned to Henry and said you know there is a possible work around for the grand unification theory

Henry said I thought you said it couldn't be done, Zandroe return to etching out the possible secret passage door, while Eva folded her arms across her chest and watched Zandroe critically, *A* looked at Eva and Zandroe her eyes narrowed then she said quietly to *D* bait and switch I didn't realise you could be so manipulative, *D* said needs must as the devil drives, *A*'s eyes narrowed more as she looked sternly at *D* and said you haven't you wouldn't do that to me? *D* interrupted by saying not so you'd notice, *A* stood up leant over and punched *D* in the leg hard, *D* said ouch and rubbed his leg, as *A* returned to her original position while pointing an accusing finger at *D* saying I'd better not notice, as a pained confused look enveloped her face as she realized those words weren't quite right somehow, in her frustration she stabbed the accusing finger at *D* again saying got it, *D* raised his hands in surrender repeating got it, *D* said did you notice how the anger clouded your mind just then, *A* said I know I know it's just you can be so infuriating at times, *D* smiling said thank you

Zandroe to *A* said do you hit him a lot? *A* said not as much as he deserves, the man's a Oxo I couldn't hurt him if I tried, and if he wanted to stop me he could easily, he's ridiculously fast despite his size, I've tried sparring with him once I hit nothing but air, and as I became more frustrated he started laughing at me, I never sparred with him again, Zandroe said martial arts? *A* said yes I train using mixed martial arts for fitness and to vent, he was a professional break dancer it's a spinoff of that kopaira or capoeira or something I can't quite remember, it's a Brazilian martial art I think, I've seen vid's it was entertaining and baffling but I couldn't see initially, how this gymnastic dancing around was any kind of martial art, there was no contact no hitting no kicking no throws, just the appearance that it was about to take place but didn't, then bang done and it was all over in a second, it dawned on me it was a martial art of deception, Zandroe said all warfare is based on deception, a quote from Sun Tzu and the art of war, *A* said yes I've listened to the audio book, it's a good book with a bad title, as he starts the book off by saying don't do it, war is wasteful destructive and horrific, perhaps a better title would have been ... war don't do it, but if you have to, this is how to do it properly, with the fewest casualties on your side, Zandroe smiled and said perhaps that is a better title, but it's not so catchy.

Henry said to *D* so? *D* repeated so? Henry said the grand unification theory the theory of everything, that you said couldn't be done, and now you're saying it can, *D* said ho yes that, wait a second "you said couldn't be done" pointing out that the universe itself does not operate on an abstract logical based finger counting mathematical system, is not some flippant "I said", it is ... thus, it has been demonstrated quod erat demonstrandum QED, unless you have found any flaws in my reasoning yes, Henry said not at this particular moment in time, but you said it could be done, *D* said I said "there is a possible work around for the grand unification theory" possible yes ... possible work around, follow me on this and tell me when you get dizzy, Isaac Newton invented gravity and discovered cat flaps, Henry in a dry tone said very funny

D continued to say, so you have gravity the attracting force between two objects, mass distance all that funky stuff yes, Henry said directly proportional to mass and inversely proportional to the square of the distance between the masses, *D* said yeah, and then you've got Einstein's dent in space time right, Henry slightly impatiently said yes the visibly observable lens effect all of this is empirically confirmed, are you going to suggest otherwise? *D* said nope not exactly it's perhaps a different way of looking at things, jigsaw puzzle pieces, gravity has a constant value yes, and then Henry said yes would you like to hear its value? *D* said six point six seven something newton metre per whatever, Henry said six point six seven three, *D* said whatever the important thing here, is that it is fixed, Henry said yes it's fixed and that's empirically confirmed, *D* said next piece of the puzzle, gravitational waves, Henry said gravitational waves yes predicted by Einstein and also empirically confirmed, *D* said waves, so we are living in a fluidique universe?

Henry scratched his chin and said now there's a leap, I really haven't thought about it that way, perhaps we are, *D* said and as we have empirically confirmed gravitational waves, that mean's gravity has not got a constant value as gravitational waves must cause fluctuations, cause and effect yes, Henry said yes but those fluctuations might be too small to measure, the equipment needed to measure gravitational waves was hypersensitive, *D* said and realistically nobody wants to upset the mathematical modelling status quo, by turning fixed into variables, if you have variable gravity and variable speed of light, you might as well take the whole physics department and throw it out of the window, and then wait for a not so predictable thud, Henry said and nobody would support that; nobody. *D* said true but let's think dangerously, what if the fluidique universe put's a new twist on thing's, so you don't just get a fixed dent in space, but gravitational waves and gravitational whirlpools, so the fixed dent has an additional attractive and repulsive elements to it, a variable depending upon the spin of the object, not as in spin up or spin down quantum state, but an actual mechanical spin, like a whirlpool in the river yes

Henry said the repulsive elements? I can see how the whirlpool would draw stuff towards its centre but the repulsive elements? *D* said for every action, Henry finish the sentence there is an opposite an equal reaction, *D* said black holes, Henry said where is this going? *D* said like I said stay with me, so a black hole ain't no hole, it's just a big Sun that's collapsed in on itself and has become such a gravitational monster, that not even light can escape its gravitational clutches, and they spin, oh boy do they spin, heading towards the speed of light spin, and that's one big fast moving whirlpool, now Henry if you had one big rubber mat on a nice shiny floor, and you started twisting the centre of that mat, Henry tentatively said then the mat itself would start moving, *D* said the mat is the fabric or fluidique medium of the universe yes, and the whirlpool is moving that medium, the universe itself yes, the whirlpool draws close objects in while simultaneously pushing distant objects out, action reaction yes

D raised one hand opening his fingers in a spreading motion and said puff there goes the need for dark energy, still with me Henry? Henry said this is cosmology; I have a keen interest but it's not exactly my specialized subject

Zandroe said this dent in space time? Shouldn't there be an anti-dent if every action has an opposite an equal reaction? *D* said got me there, I was thinking of space time as a kind of non-Newtonian fluid, I suppose adding an object would cause displacement in the space time ooze, what do you think Henry?

Henry said I think I need a degree in cosmology and astrophysics, *D* said Newton and Einstein didn't have those, and they muddle through, with just their minds and nowhere near the empirical data we have, Henry said yes but they were Newton and Einstein, and I'm not, *D* said they were just men standing on the shoulders of giants, jump up the view is fine, Henry said it's also scary and disorientating, *D* said true and it can also drive you completely insane, but what a time to go mad, Henry said I'm starting to worry about you, D said and I haven't even gotten to the good bit yet, and what I've told you so far should down-scale nicely to the quantum yes, Henry said I'd like to see the equations behind it, *D* said the empirical, the equations can be shoehorned in later, by the bean counters, until a new mathematical language can describe it more accurately yes, Henry said I am a bean counter.

D said Henry your only limits mentally are self-imposed, live a little, while we still have time yes, James said given your everything about us can be explained by evolution theory, wouldn't those mental limits be there for an evolutionary reason? *D* said yep they are there to stop you going mad.

James said Nietzsche if you stare too long into the abyss, the abyss will stare back at you, and the wisdom of Silenus, oh miserable ephemeral race, children of chance and suffering, why do you compel me to say to you what would be most beneficial for you not to hear? What is best of all is utterly unreachable, not to be born, not to be, to be nothing. But the second best for you is – to die soon

D said nicely quoted, and utterly true, to see the unvarnished reality of reality is to step into the abyss of madness and utter despair, a true Edvard Munch the scream gig, we all create delusional bubbles to save ourselves from the unvarnished horror of reality.

Zandroe said and you delight in bursting those bubbles, *D* said everybody has to have a hobby, Zandroe said I'm not going to be seventy-four on your list, but I think Junia may be correct in her assessment of you, *D* said and the truth will set you free ?

Junia said don't you dare quote the bible, *D* said to Zandroe for mankind as a species to truly evolve, all the bubbles need to be burst to unlock our true potential yes, Zandroe said the horror of reality the utter despair the madness? *D* said the utter joy and ecstasy, the enlightenment, these are two sides of the same coin, the good and the bad, both must be embraced yes, Zandroe said you're a dangerous man, *D* smiled and said thank you.

James said I don't think that was a compliment, and I think he may be right about you

Daisy said we will evolve through technology and gene manipulation, we will merge with machines, and become immortal god's, *D* said to Zandroe should I burst Daisy's delusional bubble, Daisy said it's not delusional, *D* then continued to say to Zandroe, or Emily's genocidal overpopulation bubble, *D* waved his hands, and said yes the bubbles are there for a reason yes, and if I did burst them new ones would instantly appear, you have to want to step through that fire knowing it could easily consume you, before any real damage could be done, the dangerous stuff is purely voluntary, with the very high attrition rate, Zandroe said but you did it, *D* said perhaps maybe, I can't be certain ... certainty goe's out of the window, when you look into the abyss I think yes, would you like to know how to do it? Zandroe firmly said no.

Daisy said I'd like to know, Emily interjected by saying you still haven't shown me that the world isn't, wasn't overpopulated

D smiled again and said to Emily, the argument if you strip away the look how crowded the cities are becoming, this is a resource based argument yes, Emily said yes if a well can only provide drinking water for one hundred people, then it can only provide drinking water for one hundred people, if you have any more people then everybody suffers, it's not a complicated argument, *D* said the premise of the argument is having a fixed resource, and an argument about a fixed resource of water on a planet that's surface is seventy per cent water, is somewhat blinkered yes, there's desalination or you could pull the moisture straight out of the air, or you could just dig a new well, the fixed resource argument always fails to take into account, human ingenuity, and the ability to get or create new resources when necessary, and that's why every single Domesday the end is nigh prediction of disastrous overpopulation ever, has been completely and utterly wrong, in every applicable sense of the word wrong yes

Emily said then why are people still dying of thirst and hunger?

D said politics corruption and exploitation, some dictator in some primitive backwater, that is more than happy to help engineer the circumstances then watch and invite the western media to watch his own people die of thirst and hunger, so that the western media can beat its chest in indignant rage, at the rating boosting, and revenue increasing images of poor starving children, and as the charity bosses rub their hands together in glee, while picking out their new mid-life crisis sports car, in anticipation of the fortune heading their way, and that dictator will literally be drooling over what remains of that charity money filling the coffers of their own Swiss bank account, oh how those Swiss bankers must love starving babies, Emily said what made you so cynical, *D* said life, it's not an overpopulation of people, it's an overpopulation of heartless parasitic exploiters, that's the problem

Emily said there are measures in place to stop that kind of behaviour, *D* sarcastically said sure and it's so affective, Emily's face wrinkled and she said there's just no talking to you, then she turned her head away.

D turned to Zandroe and said, there you go, not one bubble burst, when faced with reality, people automatically shy away to their delusional bubbles of comfort, and that's OK that's how society works for most people.

Zandroe said but, *D* said but most people, is a slowly but surely dwindling number, humanity is evolving yes

Daisy said I'd like to know how to look into the abyss, an old diminutive man with a sunken weathered face and drooping jowls firmly said no you wouldn't.

Henry to *D* said Lord Grace Daisy's grandfather, *D* said Lord ... Lord? The word brings to mind paedophilia tax dodging expense fiddling, you know that kind of thing, we have met before but not formally, *D* waved his hand and smiled at Lord Grace, Lord Grace turned his head slowly, and eyed *D* as a new, saying where not all like that, then he said have we met before? *D* said oh no I'm sure there's one Lord somewhere that's decent, and yes I was one of the workers that helped to construct your armoured secret bunker.

The word secret bunker, ended conversations and circulated around the room

Zandroe was just about to speak to *D* as *D* cut him off by saying it's a death trap, carefully sabotaged from top to bottom.

Lord Grace his face in a forced passive nonchalant gaze said, it was independently checked, *D* said indeed the bit I was working on the Faraday cage element had sections of plastic that looked just like metal, and contained incredibly fine high resistance wire, so if say a solar flare happened that wire would break under stress turning a protective Faraday cage into a microwave oven for the unfortunate occupants, but if that wire wasn't under stress, it would pass all the test's, like I said carefully sabotaged from top to bottom

Lord Grace pretence of serenity drained from his face, as he angrily asked who? *D* said I'm not entirely sure, I should imagine the same friends that you had sabotaged yes

James almost jokingly said evolved morality?

D said James the man is a published eugenicist, and I think there would be an incredibly high probability that my other employer was a eugenicist as well yes, is helping eugenicists euthanize each other immoral? Or is that just poetic justice? James slapped his own legs laughed and said it would take a greater mind than mine to work that one out, *D* said besides the money was good, not from him but the client paying for the additional services, but I could have done without the frets to life and limb and my poor wife and children, James said you have a wife and children?

D said no I was given a fake background, I was only there because I've done construction before and I look the part, the real reason I was there was to plant a packet sniffer, James said packet sniffer? *D* said computers send and receive packets of information, you can covertly record and read these packets of information, the practice is called sniffing, thus packet sniffing, James slightly baffled said oh, so are you like a spy or something? *D* said no just an itinerant worker and amateur philosopher, I was just doing a favour for a friend of a friend of a friend or something.

James said you don't know? *D* said there are disorganised bands of people in the hacking community, James said so you're a hacker? *D* said no just an itinerant worker and amateur, James finished off the word philosopher

D continued to say, in my early days I had some background in helping people remove particularly stubborn spyware, low-end kiddie scripter stuff, but you get to know people blackhats, whitehats, greyhats, James said huh? *D* said a whitehat is a good hacker non-destructive type person

Emily said there are no good hackers they are all vermin.

D looked at Emily for a moment and then said, did you have any embarrassing emails revealed to the public? James smiled and nodded as Emily looked away arms folded.

James said what colour hat was that? *D* said you've got more than just a black and white and grey let me give you an example, a certain operating system had an exploit, it was spotted by an individual, and that individual dutifully reported that exploit to the operating system manufacturers, the operating system manufacturers should have addressed the issue promptly but they didn't, so the individual contacted them again and again and again, nothing happened the exploit was becoming quite widely used by some not so pleasant people, and the somewhat frustrated individual that had repeatedly reported the exploit, then wrote a kind of virus designed not to harm the computer in any way whatsoever, but it was designed to crash that certain operating systems very own website, by using the very exploit he had repeatedly warned them about, the virus spread, the website crashed and then that certain operating system manufacture decided to close the exploit in an update, the press contacted the operating system manufacture, and they were told by the manufacture it was an evil malicious hacker, the press accepted one of their main advertising affiliates statement as absolute fact with no need to check or question anything, in true unbiased investigational journalism mainstream style, and restated the manufacture press release word for word as absolute fact in there news reports, now you tell me what colour hat do you think that mainstream press reported evil malicious hacker should wear?

James said gold, *D* said anyhow's Lord Grace was paying a lot of money for internet security, word got around as it does yes, and if somebody was trying very hard to hide something, James finished the sentence then the hacking community wanted to know what that was.

D continued to say, the device I was tasked to plant surreptitiously was relatively simple, it was an excellent facsimile of a hand sized stone, it had a high gain low noise multi spectrum receiver, and it used an induction loop to draw power and transmit down the mains wire, James look confused and said in simple English? *D* said that was simple English, *D* pondered for a while and then said I put a magical spy device, in his rock garden, then *D* asked James do you know nothing of electronics. James said I just use electronic devices I don't know how they work, James continued to say we can't all be geniuses you know, *D* said yes you can, the potential is within all of us, James said perhaps but we have lives to lead, we don't all have the time or the energy to pursue every subject under the Sun

D said ure a philosopher thinking up excuses for not thinking yes, James laughed then said my behaviour is all part of your evolution explains everything about us theory I'm sure, *D* said are you taking the stoic deterministic or thermodynamic paradigm in that statement? James said the confused paradigm I can't keep up with you.

Then James said you still haven't explained why you did this, for a friend of a friend of a friend you don't actually know, *D* said anonymity is part of the culture of the disorganised group, it's just the way it is in a surveillance state, I surreptitiously investigated Lord Grace found out he was a useless genocidal parasite, undoubtedly up to no good, so I was happy to play along

Emily said he's a good man, and he does a lot of charity work.

D said sure just like that dictator in some primitive backwater, does a lot of charity work.

Emily firmly said he's a good man

D looked away from Emily and slowly said whatever.

Lord Grace stood up fists clenched face full of anger, and behind gritted teeth he said to *D* you sabotaged my home you spied on me and my family, WHO PUT YOU UP TO THIS! *D* calmly said we're you not paying attention, I said I don't know, and I certainly don't care, you're a parasitic eugenicist and you've openly and financially supported the move towards the surveillance state we all now live in, so your fragile glass bubble of hypocrisy doesn't warrant any genuine outrage, less it shatters inwardly yes, so stop being a cry-bully-baby because others have done unto you what you have done unto them yes, besides even if you had that information, what exactly would you do with it ? Send those security goons in the car outside round to break some legs, by the way the car and the goons have gone, they didn't come in here to rescue you, they jumped in the car and rescued themselves, they drove past me and *A* in a hurry as we were running down the street, and that panic button you've been pressing since we got in here ain't gonna do you no good, they ain't coming back.

Lord Grace looked to his left hand clenched fist and pocketed the panic device after giving it one last press, as he put an effort into calming himself down, then he attempted but failed to project a nonchalant manner as he said, I'm a powerful man with many resources, help will be on the way.

D laughed then Lord Grace anger and fury could not be contained by a thin facade of control, and he spat out I've crushed little men like you before, *D* laughed again while saying what all eight stone nothing of you? Then while holding up his hands in mock surrender *D* said somebody help me this eight stone weakling is going to crush me, with his fragile little hands.

There were giggles from around the room.

Lord Grace looked at those giggling with daggers in his eyes, his face purple with unbridled rage, Emily was about to say something but stopped herself and she started giggling

Eva said you're a wicked man *D*, *D* smiling wickedly said and I thot I had a halo above me head, Eva said if you've got something above your head it would be short and pointy and there'd be two of them, all that talk of morality pha, *D* said just because I can define morality, this doesn't necessarily mean I'm the world's best practitioner of it yes

Zandroe smiling said ain't that the truth, *D* said truth, is the truth moral or immoral? Have I said anything that's untrue? Zandroe looked confused, James said it's not just about being truthful, *D* said so the truth won't set you free? *D* looked at Lord Grace and said why don't you sit down and calm down old man before you give yourself an aneurysm, we wouldn't want your decaying corpse stinking up the place now would we.

James said, now there's no need to talk to him like that.

D said this repugnant old eugenicist that's just threatened to crush me with his power, and he did say he's done this before yes, I should speak kindly to him less I upset his delicate sensibilities yes? James pulled a face, *D* continued to say, you lot may have taken his money, or sycophantically snuggled up to is stench for whatever gain, and then deluded yourselves with poetic bullshit, like the greater good or whatever, I certainly ain't the greatest practitioner of morality, yet my moral compass is strong enough to determine that the truth is good, and yes James it can be hurtful or used as a sadistic weapon, the truth is often unpleasant It evokes realisation and change, and we are as a species averse to change, we prefer conformity the comfort of wallowing in the repeated ritualistic stagnated bullshit of social life, and yes those that evoke change by speaking the truth are usually vilified and demonized, like me now yes

James said yes but all I meant was, shouldn't we be civil towards each other?

D said so we can all wallow comfortably in conformist bullshit? That's your life not mine James, I burst those delusional bubbles you cling to like a drowning child yes, James hesitated, and Emily said we should be civil towards each other, it's the decent thing to do, *D* laughed and said you're a eugenicist like Lord Grace, that's the polar opposite of civil towards each other yes

Emily said it's for the greater good, *D* said I think, killing off the species for its own good, is certainly not the civil thing to do, it's a bat shit crazy thing to do, Emily said it's not about killing it's about population control, which will-I mean would have benefited everybody, *D* said no retarding the gene pool retard's diversity and it retards the species it's retarded, and now the population has been drastically reduced, how do you feel? Like it's a job well done the world has suddenly become a eugenicists' utopian paradise or do you feel small weak and afraid?

Emily turned away

D said civility is born of respect, you can disagree with somebody's ideas yet still respect them as a person, and we have the surface bullshit civility that we all must endure yes, let's not confuse the two, I have no respect for Lord Grace the person who has just threaten me yes thus I will not be civil towards him, it is a mark of disrespect towards the actions of that person, not just his irrational ideas.

Lord Grace now seated and wiping the sweat from his brow hissed the feeling was mutual.

D towards Lord Grace said poor deluded fool, you could almost feel sorry for him almost, there was a letter to Archbishop Mandell Creighton from John Emerich Edward Dalberg, about the popes of the thirteenth and fourteenth centuries, he wrote "power tends to corrupt and absolute power corrupts absolutely, great men are almost always bad men, even when they exercise influence and not authority, still more when you superadd the tendency or the certainty of corruption by authority. There is no worse heresy than that the office sanctifies the holder of it. that is the point at which ... the end learns to justify the means" it's an enduring truth with remarkably few exceptions the likes of Marcus Aurelius have not been seen for millennia, power corrupts the mind, and this corruption inevitably leads to the fear loathing and hate of losing what power you have yes, so the paranoia sets in, trust friendship and love these are tool's that can be used against you to manipulate to subvert diminish and ultimately to take your power, you know the truth of this because this is how you subverted corrupted and diminished others to get your power, the mind twisting in on itself in ever decreasing spirals of corrupted circular reasoning.

D continue to say Lord Grace never had absolute power; he was himself merely a disposable gopher, in the illusionary pyramid of power, and now he finds that all his power was only a pyramid of cards held up by belief and nothing more.

D to Lord Grace said if only your mind wasn't so twisted and corrupted by that illusion of selfish and self-serving power, then perhaps you could think of a way out of here, but no you only have twisted and corrupted thoughts, running through that addled mind of yours, your loyal chattel have all run away yes, your chattel were loyal as long as you kept paying them or threatening them, and society was still stable, and they could go home to their families, now that's all gone, and so have your resources and rescue, all disappeared, and you're sat there physically and mentally weak, powerless useless and impudent, I can almost pity you, almost

Karl said like you must really hate that guy

D said let's just say my research on him was thorough, and if he spontaneously combusted I wouldn't piss on him to put the fire out, Karl said harsh, *D* looked around and said don't tell me none of you had an inkling?

Virtually everybody decided to thoughtfully examine their own shoes.

Lord Grace said you have no idea of power boy, or the resources I have at my disposal, I am no mere gopher, I have wealth beyond your capacity to understand, an army of mercenaries, and the ability to put them anywhere in the world at a moment's notice, I have advanced weapons technology beyond that of any countries abilities, I have advanced prototype military robots advanced prototype military drones, I even have advanced prototype satellites, I could topple governments at a whim, you have no idea of my power boy

D turned to Emily and said sweet little old man that likes to do charity work?

Karl said so old man when is this army going to rescue you? Lord Grace said my name is Lord Grace to the likes of you, even this fool as he points towards *D* addresses me by my proper title, and they will come, they will come.

D said I only use the title Lord to mean child molester tax dodger expense fiddler you know low life good for nothing parasite, it's what the title represents that's important yes, and no they won't come, armies of mercenaries drones and robots are not waiting patiently at the traffic lights, making their way very-very slowly to rescue you, that army of the infected would scare even the most hardened mercenary, and no robot could withstand the sheer multitude out there, your little tormented corrupted mind just isn't thinking straight is it, this is not to imply that your tormented corrupted mind ever did think straight yes

A said what about our mercenaries?

Zandroe said your mercenaries? Before *D* could reply, *A* said there not no, there not our mercenaries per se they are just some mercenaries we know you know, Zandroe said no I don't know, just some mercenaries you happen to know? *A* said well it's more *D* knows them and I know them through *D*

Zandroe gave *A* a look but said nothing, *A* continued to say you know *D* does his clever thinking stuff, Zandroe said yes all too well, *A* said so they come up with a plan and then pass it to *D* to see if he can find any fault with it, Zandroe said so *D* is a military strategist, *A* looked to *D* then *D* said nope just an itinerant worker and amateur philosopher, they are the military strategists I'm just an independent fault finder for them, I just know one of the team from way back, and they trust me to look at things critically, it's not that often and no money changes hands, just favours for favours *D* looked at *A* and said I'm sure scum are OK, they have the luck of the Irish

Zandroe said scum?

A said Small Cowardly Unit of Mercenaries scum, Zandroe giggled and then said scum, I don't suppose they're on their way here to rescue us? *D* said highly unlikely, but if we do make it out of here, and if we are able to contact them, and if they're still alive, and if they can get to us, then we might stand a slightly better chance of living for a few more hours, perhaps maybe, Zandroe said that's a lot of if's, *D* said ain't it just.

Then *D* continued to say, how is that trapdoor thing coming along, Zandroe said the basic outline is starting to emerge I might just squeeze through it if it actually goes anywhere, *D* said well don't let me stop you, Zandroe frowned and said I haven't worked this hard (then a puzzled look emerged across his face) then after a pause and with a slightly surprised tone in his voice he continued to say ever!

D turn to Henry and said if you look at the universe as fluidique, Zandroe interrupted by saying this whole equals MC squared thing, I don't understand it? What does it actually mean?

D turn to Zandroe and said OK you have a supernova a Sun way, way bigger than ours and it goes bang yes, are you with me so far, Zandroe hesitantly said yes, *D* said energy itself is accelerated in that explosion yes, Zandroe said OK so far *D* said that energy if it's accelerated enough it becomes matter, Zandroe said it becomes matter? *D* said yep, it's as simple as that, and if eventually in time under the right circumstances if that matter goes down a gravity well and that matter collides with other particles of matter in an environment that forces them closer and closer together, a lot of the energy it took to create the matter in the first place is released, Zandroe said so that's how atomic bombs work, boom! Zandroe gestured with his hands, *D* said yep when energy is accelerated towards the speed of light it becomes matter, Zandroe said and this is how all the matter in the universe was created at the big bang? *D* said mmm well yes-ish

Zandroe said yes-ish? *D* said well matter itself is still being created and then converted back to energy and then created again, it's probably more accurate to think of it as just energy manifesting itself in different states and the big bang singularity theory you were taught at school, isn't accurate, Zandroe said then why was I taught it at school? *D* said convenience ... and it shut you up, there are a lot of paradoxes and unanswered questions, and the authority figure at school ain't going to look very authoritative, not knowing, you should know this yourself Zandroe yes, Zandroe said so do you know?

D said nope, Zandroe said the paradoxes? *D* said gravity and time seem linked together, they may in fact be the same thing, you get time dilation a clock on the earth's surface will run a tad more slowly than a clock at high altitudes, Zandroe said yes I've heard something about this, *D* said so if gravity which is matter which is energy and if time are all the same thing, how do you get time before matter? And how do you get matter before time? And as there's no such thing as acceleration without time, and without acceleration you don't get matter, Zandroe said sounds like it's the chicken and the egg scenario, *D* said hardly that one's easy to work out yes, although for paradoxes perhaps the strangest is the double slit experiment, which I was just about to discuss with Henry

Zandroe said you've just have to explain that one, *D* said you do like your paradoxes Zandroe yes, Zandroe said who doesn't? *D* smiled and said well this for many is the mother of them all, and it's even got a fancy name, quantum duality, the greatest minds on the planet got together at Copenhagen to work this out, names like Niels Bohr and Werner Heisenberg. Max Planck, Albert Einstein and so on there is a nice picture of them altogether, Zandroe said so what is this paradox?

D said I was coming to that, I'm just giving you some background here, Zandroe said does this background go on for much longer? *D* said no, the important thing is their interpretation of the double slit experiment, which is matter exists as both a wave like a radio wave and a particle simultaneously, it occupies two states of existence thus "quantum duality" until you look at it and then it becomes either one or the other, with of course lots of accompanying technical mumbo jumbo wavefunction, wavefunction collapse and so on, Zandroe said until you look at it?

Henry said it sounds fantastical, but it's not, the observer via the act of observation collapses the wavefunction.

D said to Zandroe technical mumbo jumbo? Zandroe said technical mumbo jumbo, *D* said anyhow's, the double slit experiment, works like this you get a piece of cardboard plastic metal whatever you cut two little slits somewhere near the middle, then you fire bits of matter at it, light electron's atoms whatever, sticks some photographic paper on the other side, to see where those particles end up, and off you go, Zandroe said I could have done this at home? *D* said yep, Zandroe said so where is the mother of all paradoxes? *D* said, what would you expect to see? Zandroe said I don't understand? *D* said just scale it up in your mind, you have an old castle wall with two arrow slits in it, and behind that a billboard sign that's completely white, and in your hand you have a rapid fire paintball gun, Zandroe said I've tried paintball it hurts and I'm too big a target, *D* laughed and then said you let rip with your rapid fire paintball gun at the old castle wall with two arrow slits in it, what would you expect to see on the other side where the billboard is? Zandroe said there all lined up? *D* said yep

Zandroe thought for a moment then said this isn't a trick question? *D* said nope, Zandroe said I'd expect to see two lines of paint on the billboard roughly in the shape of the arrow slits unless the arrow slits are close together then it would just be a mess, *D* said exactly, so what would you expect to see in a scaled down version with photons electrons and such? Zandroe said the same but I'm guessing it's not, *D* said you're guessing correctly, there're multiple lines, interference lines also known as wave patterns, Zandroe said the paintballs are obviously bouncing off each other, this is no great paradox, *D* said but the particles are being fired one at a time to avoid this, and it still producers the interference lines, Zandroe said how is that possible? *D* said the generally accepted explanation is wave particle duality, the particle exists as a wave of probability passes through both slits interferes with itself and then collapses into a particle and leaves its mark, but here's the twist, if you watch it happening you only ever get two lines, the experiment must be unobserved to create the wave patterns, Zandroe said this can't be true

Henry said it's all true empirically observed millions of times, Zandroe said it makes no sense, no sense at all, Henry said welcome to the world of quantum mechanics.

D said welcome to the world of celebrity scientists and scientific consensus, it is an ancient and proud practice, and it has a long and illustrious history of being absolutely wrong one hundred per cent of the time yes, Henry said so do you think it's quantum decoherence or the pilot-wave or many-worlds interpretation? *D* said nope I think it's the *D* interpretation, and virtually everybody has been looking at the whole thing in completely the wrong way, this is a fluidique universe, a particle travelling through fluidique space time will create a space time wake, the particle travels through one slit, the wake travels through both then interferes with itself, causing the interference pattern on the other side, the wake itself is a distortion of space time, and if the particle is spinning which it always is, then you end up with a twisted space time wake that appears to be an oscillating wave just like a radio wave yes, as the particle itself appears to be the wave and not the particle, a bit like partially submerging a ruler into some wavy water yes

Zandroe said that makes more sense than that other thing, Henry said don't you have some work to do Zandroe? Then Henry said to *D* and the wavefunction collapse, and the observer? *D* said it's a wakefunction collapse, the particle appears to be in multiple places, and technically it is until the space time distortion wake catches up with itself, and the wake, like all wake's has a kinetic influence on space time, the observer ... The observer is still problematic, obviously there is some catalytic effect.

Zandroe said catalytic effect? Henry gave Zandroe a look, Zandroe ignored it, *D* to Zandroe said picture during the days when cars were driven by people, in England they tried speed matrix sign's, it would show your speed on a flashing high visibility display, Zandroe said I remember those, *D* continued to say, most people would see this then realise they were driving too fast and slow down, they also tried this in Russia but it had the opposite effect, the sign was acting as a catalyst, it speeded up the cars just by being there, the sign didn't say go faster or slower, it didn't increase the horsepower of the cars, although its mere presence was a catalyst for a reaction yes

Zandroe said so an observer has a catalytic effect on matter? *D* said matter energy space time yes an observable effect

Emily said are you a spiritual man *D*? Henry Zandroe and *D* rolled their eyes then *D* said I try very hard not to be, Emily said but what you're saying about the observer fits

D facepalmed then he said the evidence fits some theory you have? Emily said perhaps, *D* said that's the wrong way of thinking, then *D* continued to say, spiritualism is belief without evidence, except when scientific evidence appears to reinforce whatever believe you have, then it is eagerly accepted, when scientific evidence contradicts those believes it is ignored or dismissed, spiritualism itself forwards no evidence ever, for it is belief without evidence, and that's the wrong way of thinking yes, Emily said there are more things in heaven and earth, Horatio, than are dreamt of in your philosophy.

Eva almost to herself said is there a Hamlet theme developing here?

D casually glanced at Eva and then *D*'s gaze fell upon Emily then *D* dramatically quoted, "thee ghost to Scrooge said why do you doubt your senses? Because said Scrooge a little thing affects them, a slight disorder of the stomach makes them cheats, you may be an undigested bit of beef, a blot of mustard, a crumb of cheese, a fragment of an underdone potato, there's more of gravy than of grave about you, whatever you are !"

Eva quietly said humbug.

Zandroe said how about a non-food conversation if you please, this is awakening my appetite, *D*'s gaze fell upon Zandroe and he gave him a look.

Then *D*'s gaze return to Emily and he said, the mind is a delicate thing that is prone to deception and especially self-deception, scientific methodology helps to ground ideas in reality, Emily said science doesn't have all the answers, *D* said I think you've got completely the wrong idea here, it's not that spiritualism is too bizarre too esoteric and is beyond the understanding of science, it ain't, me and Henry where chatting about the universe being fluidique

Henry interjected by saying you still haven't presented any evidence or described this fluidique medium, *D* said indeed I haven't, I wrongfully assumed it was obvious, the evidence is gravitational waves which are backed empirically yes, and the medium is gravity itself, or more concisely space time gravity energy as they are all one and the same thing yes

D paused for a moment then said we exist inside the non-Newtonian fluidique protomatter energy of the universe, with waves currents eddies funnel's and all that funky stuff all in constant motion, and this is all non-uniform as the waves necessarily prove variability in density and thus variability in the tensile stresses yes, you can achieve a lot by pretending gravity and the speed of light are fixed and universally uniform and constant, but I think it's time for this pretence to end yes

Henry rubbed his chin thoughtfully as he began to ponder.

D said to Emily, anyhow's me and Henry could as easily be talking about fourth dimensional quasicrystals, or non-local realism and quantum entanglement in relation to interdimensional consciousness, or a plethora of subjects so bizarre they've had to tweak the words so people overhearing scientific conversation's don't fall about laughing, spiritualism is just tame lame and unimaginative in comparison, and spiritualism equips you with neither the language nor the thinking skills required to join in the conversation, nor does spiritualism equip you with the tools to distinguish good science from bad science yes, so say if you want to reinforce your spiritual belief with science, how do you actually know if either are sound? Spiritualism is just the wrong way to think yes.

Emily said so what's the right way to think Mr know it all?

D said the principle is quite easy, the practice well that's another thing yes, the principle is clarity of thought, starting with neutral scepticism, neutscept if you will, with your own beliefs and values, this is incredibly difficult, the jump to conclusions, the easy answer confirming your own biases these are always ever present yes, but perhaps the hardest thing is taking the time to think, just think exclusively about one thing, pondering over a concept for a good long while yes, but it ain't just the thinking, unless you have the strength of will to be laughed at ridiculed ostracised if you're thinking doesn't conform with everybody else's then you should let apathy take its course, and let others do the thinking for you yes

D looked around and he spotted Ellicott *D* smiled pointed at Ellicott and then said to Emily do you believe in climate change?

Emily without hesitation said yes, *D* said what is wrong with that ad-nauseam question I've just asked? Emily opened her mouth *D* gestured at her to stop and said think about it yes.

Ellicott said it's an easy question with an easy answer if you believe in science. *D* almost rhetorically said believe in science? Is science dropping empiricism for a more esoteric faith based belief system? Can I get anointed into the church of science if I abandon my wicked unholy sinful empirical evidence based independently verified ways and become a (*D* raised his hands to his own head height and jiggled them about for dramatic effect while emphasizing the word) believer? Ellicott waved a dismissive hand laughed and turned away.

D looked at Emily and said think yes, take your sweet time and think.

John Runndolf said this is ridiculous, of course, climate science is evidence based you're being silly, *D* said have you seen the original data sheets do you have access to the model used? oh wait a second no you don't, only the anointed priests of the church of anthropogenic climate change have access to the "cough" science

Ellicott said so there are copyright issues with the original data sheets meaning they can't be freely distributed, and the models are not released because of the potential misuse issues by the crazies

D turned to John Runndolf and said, no verifiable empirical data up for your, or anybody else's independent scrutiny yes, not one jot of foundational evidence but a mountain of excuses and special pleading, you just need to believe yes, *D* again raised his hands to his own head height and jiggled them about for dramatic effect,

Ellicott said there is scientific consensus, *D* said scientific consensus it has the appearance the veneer of being scientific but well as it's entirely based on what scientists believe but can't prove

D turn to Henry and said there was scientific consensus against Einstein's relativity theory, even a book one hundred top scientists and whatever, against silly little Einstein's uneducated and unscientific theory, weren't there? Henry nodded and quoted Einstein “if I were wrong, then one author would have been enough” *D* quoted “or just one verifiable fact” then *D* said scientific consensus has a long and illustrious history, of being absolutely wrong one hundred pre...Karl shouted smoke! I smell smoke!

A said calm yourself, when you can’t smell thee toilette for smoke, then we make our move, this may not take long so prepare yourselves.

A looked at *D* and *D* looked at *A* then they nodded simultaneously.

Emily looking at *A* and *D* said what the fuck was that about? And prepare yourselves? You’ve got me thinking about shit, *D* said I’ve got you thinking yes, now it’s time to think about something more relevant to our current situation than bad science yes.

Emily said like what? *A* said your choices, *D* said I choose to have a going out gruntie, as he stood up and made his way to the makeshift toilet, Emily said what do I do? *A* said use your mind to make decisions based on the available data, how do you make decisions in politics?

Emily tilted her head to one side and gave a half smile, *A* softly laughed and said just keep thinking, the more you think the more options you have, in this chaotic situation try not to think too far ahead, you make it out of this room then what think through the possibilities the likely scenarios, Emily gave *A* a wide eyed look, *A* continued to say, and think about those that have real love for you and those who you love, think about the one’s that may betray your love and trust, if the situation becomes desperate, who will be truly for you and who will be only for their selves, Emily's eyes narrowed as she suspiciously looked around the room, and the room almost fell silent as people started looking at each other as new.

The room remained relatively quiet until *D* open the door to the makeshift toilet rentering the room

D turned and while closing the door he said to the makeshift toilet he was closing the door on, spit the bones out of that bastard, as he made his way back to his original position and while preparing to recline received a kick from *A* as she nodded towards the now quiet group.

D said have you failed to inspire the troops Joan of Arc? *D* received another kick, then he slowly straightened himself in a seated position, and clapped his hands once firmly, all eyes fell upon him he spoke slowly deliberately he said, we all feel small powerless and afraid from time to time, this should be one of those times

D gestured towards the door holding back the horde of infected and he continues to say, yet we all have power not some meaningless ethereal vague and worthless power. No, we have the power to affect the universe itself reality itself, Henry and I were discussing the observer problem earlier yes, it's a problem so big and so profound it becomes an elephant in the room of ideas and thus it escapes most people, the problem is measurable observable testable the problem is real the problem is consciousness, our consciousness affects change in the universe, our consciousness affects reality, thee realization and the consequences of this is just too much for the mind to handle, so it is rejected and not embraced, I ask you to suspend your disbelief, and to go against your natural instincts to reject what you don't understand, I ask you to embrace the power of our reality, and embrace the ability to change it yes, I ask you to fully realise our potential to collectively change reality, now ... let us meditate before we go kick another realities butt.

Emily said I knew it! I fucking knew it! *D* said you guessed it, and without that scientific language and methodology that guess can go nowhere yes, Emily said so why weren't we told? *D* smiled and said you were repeatedly; you just weren't listening yes.

Karl said I don't know how to, meditate I mean, well I just don't know how, you know like? Emily said it's easy, and she started to adopt the lotus position.

Zandroe said I hardly think sitting round and chanting like hippies will help, Emily gave Zandroe a look, *D* said meditation brings wisdom, lack of wisdom leaves ignorance, know well what leads you forward and what holds you back yes, meditation can't hurt and it may help, Zandroe shrugged

D said to Emily there's no need for the lotus position, then he turned to Karl and said it ain't easy, you have a conscious and subconscious mind, well more accurately you have a dual conscious and multiple subconscious's yes, your subconscious present's you with answers and questions as you have multiple subconscious's so you get multiple answers and questions longings desire designs schemes the whole cornucopia of what it is to be human, consciously you need to let it go yes, don't follow trains of thought do not contemplate on desires just let it all come and go, let your subconscious do its thing, and just let it go, you will become aware of your own heart beat your breathing and everything around you just let it be, do not focus in upon it let your conscious mind be still and just let it all go, sounds easy yes, but the practice, and it is practice is hard yes.

Karl said, and this will make me smarter like? *D* said that's a desire, to meditate for a desire defeats the object yes, but yes it's reputedly a side effect, but do not meditate for any reason, for there is no reason when you let it all go, Karl said I'm not sure I understand like, *D* said a true statement of wisdom, it's working already, then *D* winked and said could we have a couple of minutes of silence for those that want to meditate

CHAPTER HALF A DOZEN; AI

The room fell silent for about a minute, then Emily started chanting while rocking backwards and forwards in the lotus position, *D* facepalmed then stood up while grabbing the metal bar he had straightened earlier, he then walks towards the almost finished etched out shaped Zandroe had been working on, then he drove the metal bar right through one side wiggled the bar about making a great deal of noise, exciting the infected behind the barricaded door, then *D* drove the metal bar right through the other side repeating the process, the door holding back the infected started to creak and strain.

Eva in an exasperated manner said not so loud, *D* while pushing his foot through the top of the secret door collapsing it in way of an exclamation point said, we ain't in a library now!

D then pick up the door and threw it onto the upturned table then he strode over to the barred window, and pulled out the remaining metal bars, tossing them into the centre of the room, then with one hand holding the straightened metal bar vertical on the inside of the window he squeezed through the window to the other side using the metal bar as a brace to hold himself in place, the metal bar held *D*'s weight precariously as it slotted into the gap that was created when the bar was pulled out.

A followed *D* she picked up one of the metal bars and with a helping hand from *D* she then slipped through the window to the other side also using her metal bar as a brace, the metal bar was held more precariously in place than *D*'s the bar had not been straightened, but she weighed a lot less than *D*, while all this was going on Zandroe was transfixed with the opening that had been created so violently, Zandroe almost to himself said there are stairs, and indeed there is a narrow stone spiral staircase leading downwards, the staircase was perhaps a little too narrow for Zandroe's girth, with *D* and *A* now on the outside of the building and with Zandroe's curiosity edging him closer towards the revealed staircase

The room had become a cacophony of noise with the agitated people in the room and the agitated infected behind the now creaking and groaning barricaded door, Emily whom was now standing, as was everybody with the exception of Junia shouted towards the window, what do we do now?

D poked his head through the window and said, make life or death decisions yes.

Then *D* and *A* uncoupled the bars they were using to brace themselves then pulled the metal bars through the window dropped them to the ground and made their way via an extremely narrow ledge towards a drainpipe

Eva reached into her handbag retrieved a torch turned it on, she told Zandroe to move and started to make her way down the narrow, spiral stone staircase

Karl made his way partly through the window, and saw *D* grab hold of the drainpipe then *D* helped *A* to also grab hold of it, *A* motioned Karl to stop, then she pointed to an industrial sized wheelie bin, Karl nodded and held his position, and he relayed the information to those on the inside.

James went for the stairway patting Zandroe on the back as he pushed by him, James looked Zandroe up and down then he said, I think it's probably best if you go last.

D and *A* where pushing the industrial wheelie bin over warn cobblestones towards the window, the cobblestones glistened and sparkled as light reflected and refracted from the quartz crystals within the stones, the light danced through droplets of mist and smoke as they moved across the courtyard, *A*'s bare feet and *D*'s formal shoes held little traction and the pair struggled in their task, the courtyard looked originally designed for coach and horses, a large wide archway, with wooden gate's at its entrance, the wooden gate had a gap of perhaps three or four inches from the ground, and at the top a relatively straight line of wood with protruding metal spikes starting at the base of the archway curve, leaving a gap of perhaps three to four feet at the archway curved apex, the gates were perhaps twelve to fifteen feet high, the walls of this archway protruded backwards towards the struggling pair, the courtyard was an upside down L shape, with a large section of wall following the street on the other side, and leading towards its hypotenuse was what looked like stables converted into a garage

While *D* and *A* manoeuvred the industrial sized wheelie bin into position locked the wheels and *D* had jumped up on top of the bin and was helping Karl down, *A*'s attention was drawn to a small moving dark patch that had lodged itself under the wooden barred gate's she slowly hesitantly move towards it

Lord Grace and Daisy also John the desk clerk and Junia were arguing over which way to go, John Runndolf was the next out of the window followed by Emily George Henry Francis Bertrice and Ellicott, James had already gone down the stairway following Eva, Daisy went out of the window despite Lord Grace protestations and attempt to physically stop her by grabbing her dangling legs as she pushed her own body through the window, this attempt to physically stop her was met with a kick that floored the old man, he half recovered himself shaking a bony fist at his disappearing granddaughter, while shouting I disinherit you, do you hear me I disinherit you ! You stupid bitch you fucking stup … his words were interrupted by the sharp crack of wood snapping, as one of the beams in the wooden door holding back the infected, had given way.

Junia let out a seriously high pitched blood curdling scream

A turned sharply around from her slow movement towards the arched gate, to look at the window where the scream was emanating from, then she looked at the small group that were all looking at the window, *D* jumped down from the bin, quickly unlock the wheels then started pushing the bin towards the street wall, the group started objecting some because there were still people up there, some because they were being physically pushed out of the way, *A* was caught betwixt and between, her curiosity about what had just lodged itself under the gate, and her fear of what was going to be coming through the window next

Lord Grace frozen for a moment in panic collected himself stood up, and walked over to Zandroe who was frozen transfixed on the broken beam of wood trapped partly in place by the wooden bar and upturned table, Zandroe could see glimpses shadows of the frenetic stifled movement of the infected behind, as the wood itself was jostled at a hypnotic speed, then the wood cracked in succession as Lord Grace slapped Zandroe in the face, then in a stern and uncompromising manner said to Zandroe, follow me!

Zandroe looked confused and overwhelmed then he received another slap from Lord Grace who said, NOW! The lights went back on in Zandroe's eyes and he nodded, Lord Grace turned on his phone's light and slipped into the narrow stairway followed by Zandroe

Zandroe was struggling with the narrow passage and a few steps in became stuck, Zandroe said this is worse than squeeze belly alley, then he said help I'm stuck! Lord Grace who was deliberately walking slowly in front of Zandroe, turned around moved the phone from his left hand to his right walked back towards Zandroe removing with his free hand a stylish glinting metal pen from his inside breast jacket pocket, and in a calming reassuring tone said let me help you, then with all the force he could muster he stabbed Zandroe deep in the eye with the pen, the pen reached Zandroe's brain and he went into schisms, as Lord Grace wiped the pen clean on Zandroe's jacket then he said hold the fort here old chap, and he moved briskly down the stairs

John the desk clerk was now standing in a fighting stance covering Junia position, Junia was crying whimpering and rocking in the seated fetal position in the corner, most of the beams of wood were now dislodged the wooden bar was straining and the upturned table was starting to wiggle its way downwards, John the desk clerk said fuck this, turned around grabbed Junia whom instantly screamed and resisted at his touch, he manhandled her towards the window and looked out to see *D* sat astride the street wall helping the group clamber over the bin and then lowering them to the other side while John Runndolf was helping to hold the bin in place, John the desk clerk looked down at the drop from the window then he dragged Junia kicking and screaming towards the stairway to encounter Zandroe's twitching body blocking the passage a few steps in, John the desk clerk pushed Zandroe's body as hard as he could but this only wedged Zandroe more tightly in place, John the desk clerk yelled MOVE YOU FAT FUCKING FUCK ! At Zandroe's body

Junia released from John the desk clerk's grasp retreated to her original corner and returned to weeping sobbing and rocking in the seated fetal position, while John the desk clerk was beating Zandroe's body, John the desk clerk turned around resolved to risk the fall from the window, fists clenched red faced full of anger fear and frustration, then the wooden bar door imploded, the upturned table had wiggled its way down and offered no more resistance, the wooden bar under the strain exploded with shards and splinter's flying through the room like angry insects looking for victims, followed closely by the hoard of infected

D and John Runndolf were both sitting astride the wall when

Junia's final scream was cut short, they simultaneously looked towards the window where that final interrupted scream came from, to see the light in the window blocked out as the infected dropped from the window

D and John Runndolf in unison kicked the bin away from the wall and then lowered themselves to the street side, while the bin moved about four feet as it jarred and danced against the warn cobblestones then it toppled over.

Eva had reached the bottom of the spiral stone staircase, and was confronted with an old rusty iron bar gate, and beyond what looked like roman sewers laid out horizontal to their position, James had caught up to her, and they were both struggling with a rusty latch, fragments of the noise conversations snapping wood and screams echoed down to them, instilling frantic haste into their task, although they just managed to get in each other's way.

Eva firmly grasped one of the iron bars and shook the gate vigorously while in an exasperated manner said to James just let me do this, I do not require your help, the shaking worked the latch was lifted, and they both entered the sewer Eva gave a smug self-satisfied huff while doing this, James asked which way? And in the few moments of silence that question was being considered, they both turned as they both heard footsteps heading downwards towards them, the footsteps were not frantic or panicked, but Eva and James suddenly were, despite their momentary relief at opening the iron bar gate moments earlier, they both let out a sigh of relief at the sight of Lord Grace, but this then raised the question where is Zandroe? And the others where are they?

Lord Grace explained somewhat breathlessly, that there was only Zandroe behind him everybody else had exited through the window, Zandroe had become trapped thee infected who had broken through the door, were being held back by nothing more than Zandroe's bulk, Eva said you mean, then she paused

Lord Grace said yes, now we must hurry, Eva asked James for his house keys, James put his hand in his pocket, then paused with a bemused look upon his face, Lord Grace entered the sewer and closed the iron bar gate behind him while Eva was asking for James house keys, Eva's facial expression and demeanour had taken on that of a school mistress asking a naughty petulant child to hand over whatever it was hiding

Eva said in a somewhat sarcastic manner, any time today James, thrusting out her open palm further towards James, James obliged by handing over his keys, with a somewhat confused look upon his face, Eva snatched the keys eagerly out of James hand, then she moved nudging Lord Grace out of the way towards the latch on the iron bar gate, just below the latching mechanism were two pieces of metal one connected to the wall, one was part of the gate itself, they had overlapping holes originally designed for some kind of padlock, Eva fumbling slightly to place the largest key over the two adjoining holes, which were a fraction too small to accept the key through them, then she used the butt of her torch to force the issue.

James confusion disappeared and realizing what was happening, he said my keys! Eva turned to say to James, do you think you're going home to tea and biscuits? Wake up or die Mr philosopher, then she reached inside her tweed jacket pocket removed a tissue paper, scrunched it up and threw it into the dark murky waters of the sewer, she then observed the movement of the paper and exclaimed, this way, nudging Lord Grace back up against a wall as she brushed by him on the narrow ledge of the sewer.

Lord Grace said she's got her fasci on, and it's off to the enclosures, then Lord Grace followed Eva, James looked at his keys wedged into the iron gates locking mechanism, then looked at Eva and Lord Grace and the only light source's disappearing as they scurried away, with the darkness starting to fall about him, James gave his keys one last look and then followed Eva and

Lord Grace, hurrying himself along to catch up.

The group outside of range of whatever device was being used to jam phone signals and Wi-Fi usage, well their devices awoke in a cacophony of sound

A had made her way to where the two metal bars had previously been slung over the street wall, she was squatting shoes in one hand, one of the metal bars in the other, *D* strode over towards her, then *A* with all the effort she could muster tossed one of the metal bars into the air towards *D*

D caught the metal bar midway along its horizontal axis spun it around and while going into a one leg kneeling position slammed the end of the metal bar against the ground, the sound startled those milling around texting and making phone calls, *A* had already picked up the other metal bar and was heading for *D*'s position, she clambered upon his back to adopt the piggy-back riders position

D using a metal bar he was holding as a brace stood up and started to walk in the direction away from the street entrance of the merchant house, saying to *A* here we go again, *A* dangling her heels in front of his face said but this time no spurs

The street itself looked eerily nonchalant apart from the spectacle of *D* and *A* and the amber red glow of the distant fires shimmering through the mist and smoke, it was just an ordinary narrow one way street with high walls and windowless buildings either side, there was no visible signs of the chaos that had rampaged along it earlier, *D* and *A* separated themselves from the group, and as the piggyback team ambulated towards the end of the street

Emily looked up from her phone and called out, you just can't leave us here!

D's voice echoed back, yes I can.

As the now somewhat shadowy piggyback figure of *D* and *A*

partly obscured by the midst and smoke turned the corner and disappeared, while Emily had called out to them the noise of the group who had momentarily quietened as the group had stopped playing with their phones to watch the spectacle of *D* and *A* disappearing, and while the chatter and noise from the phones subsided to almost nothing

The noise of the sniffing behind the wall they were milling around came into sharp focus, Francis snatched Bertrice's phone right out of her hand and threw it over the wall, Bertrice in an agitated protest said what do you think you are doing? Francis said saving your life, he grabbed her arm and started pulling her in the direction *D* and *A* had disappeared, Bertrice indecisively resisted at first looking towards the direction her phone had just been thrown, saying, but my phone, Francis said fuck your phone, and pulled harder forcing Bertrice along less she fell over from the exerted force on her arm

Emily was trotting along in her pink heels trying to keep up with them while still texting and the rest of the group followed like herd animals.

Francis and Bertrice caught up to *D* and *A* and stopped short to find themselves confronted by two metal bars pointed menacingly at them, *A* looked Francis up and down then said arr the man emerges, *A* moved her metal bar horizontally and motioned to throw it down to Francis, Francis instinctively released his grip from Bertrice arm and adopted a catch position, *A* nodded then Francis nodded and *A* tossed the metal bar down for Francis to catch, then *A* said to Francis make yourself useful, then *A* said to *D* that was getting heavy, then *A* said here are the rest of them, out for a Sunday evening window-shopping promenade

Although that Sunday evening window-shopping promenade came to a halt at the realization at all the devastation surrounding them, all the visible windows were smashed, cars were flattened as if some monstrously oversized Victorian steamroller as wide as the road itself had cut a swathe along this thoroughfare, there were tattered pieces of clothing caught upon the jagged edges of the crushed reinforced thermoplastic of the car chassis, sparks sizzles and small fires from the crushed car batteries and super-capacitors now exposed to oxygen, adding more smoke to the apocalyptic scene of devastation

Karl's mouth opened, phone in his hand dangling by his side he said smakjaw int'it.

A manoeuvred *D*'s head towards a smashed burglar alarm about fifteen feet above the ground, and then another smashed burglar alarm slightly further along this shop front street, the others instinctively followed *A* and *D*'s gaze upwards, *A* quietly said I think they are sound phobic

All were silent trying to work out how those alarms were smashed, *D* said Ꙧedved could you turn off the audio notifications on all phones in this cell area?

Ꙧedved's voice with a heavy Russian accent came out of all the phones the group were holding, he said sure I'm not busy it's not like there's a zombie apocalypse or anything going on, turn the fucking things off yourself

D said to the group could you turn your phones off please, Emily said if we turn our phones off we won't receive notifications and you won't be able to communicate with your friend, she lowered her voice and said I think he may be Russian

Ꙧedved laughed then said not too bright I think, but very pretty

D said turn them off, or start walking in the opposite direction now yes, *D* pointed towards the smash burglar alarm and said, hashtag emoji audio notifications will get you killed frowny face, but if you are dying for an automated notifications that will get your dumbasses killed I'd rather you did it as far away from me as possible angry face

Emily said I am not a dumbass!

D said given our circumstances you are all making a prize winning impersonation yes, just turn the fucking phone off!

Emily said OK OK and fumbled to turn her phone off as did the others who had phones, *D* and *A* watched them turn their phones off, and roll them up and put them away, then *D* said don't be surprised by what happens next yes.

Then *D* said are the phones off 𝔐edved? 𝔐edved's voice came from the phone's he said checking, at which point the group acted surprised and started to pull their phones out, *D* and *A* in her piggyback position upon *D*'s shoulders simultaneously face-palmed.

Emily said I don't understand my phone was off, *D* to Emily said surprised? Emily instinctively said yes as her attention was drawn to her phone now powering up

D said slowly as if talking to a small obstinate child said, don't be surprised by what happens next yes, now turn the fucking phone off again and don't be surprised by what happens next.

Emily said I don't understand *D* said that statement is the beginning of all wisdom yes, but now is the time for action, not a town council debating seminar, Karl the only one with a phone not to check if it was in fact off, said your phone never actually turns off like, Emily said no. Then she said why? Karl was about to answer but *D* motioned him to stop and repeated now is not the time for a town council debating seminar.

The phones that had been turned off and then checked by turning them on and turned off again, all were again stowed away

𝔐edved said all off, then he said and where did you get this bunch of zombie fodder? *D* said oh this is the cream of the crop, the intellectual master race, whom look down upon the great unwashed masses, the proletariat the likes of you and I 𝔐edved, 𝔐edved laughed then said oh their here to save the day as soon as they update their vacuous social account, about the mentally incompetent proletariat, while the apocalypse is happening all around them, how could we survive this apocalypse without a cutting remark about what we poor ignorant proletariat don't understand regarding the finer and very important and meaningful politically correct niceties about .... Whatever, *D* said you're just not being inclusive and progressive 𝔐edved, and that kind of attitude is not helpful during a zombie apocalypse, they both laughed, then 𝔐edved said talking about helpful I have a package for you and *A* on its way, and oh there's, no, no gotta go, then there was just the background noise of the street

D and *A* the piggyback team turned around and started walking carefully along the street of broken glass, Emily scrunch her face up as if holding back a torrent of abuse ready to be unleashed, but she held her tongue and followed as did the rest, they passed betting shops charity shops more charity shops a convenience shop an international food shop without incident, all with broken windows all having the look of being ramshackled by a force of nature

Then *D* and *A* stopped at an army and navy shop *A* said bug out bag joyfully

Emily said what's a bug out bag? As *A* and *D* where performing acrobatics so that *A*'s bare feet didn't touch the ground of broken glass, and they could both enter the shop, Karl to Emily said a bug out bag is you know, a bag for bug-ing out like, for when you know the lights go out, there is a meteor strike earthquake flood zombie apocalypse some kind of disaster, and you need to head for the hills like, so you have sum-ing to start fires hunt purify water you know like

D and *A*'s somewhat comical acrobatics finished, with *A* being somewhat unceremoniously carried under one of *D*'s arms into the shop, followed by Emily Karl and the rest

Emily to Karl said a survival bag? Karl said yer exactly like, Emily said but the government already has contingency plans and equipment, all ready to use in any disaster, you don't need a bug out bag, Karl sarcastically said yer like, then he spread his arms out and said well here's the disaster where is the government and its plans and equipment like? Karl held one hand above his eyes as if to shield them from the Sun then he said I don't see em Miss town councillor, and if you were in one of those government buildings, I wouldn't be seeing you now would I like, you'd be all tucked away in a taxpayer funded bug out shelter init, like specifically designed not to be used under any circumstances by the taxpayer's like

While this discussion was going on, Emily had become somewhat distracted watching *A* as she was placed by the shoe rack, and *D* as he grabbed himself a pair of black cargo trousers some insoles a pair of socks and some eighteen hole military boots and was in the process of putting them all on, *A* had also grabbed herself some insoles a pair of socks and some eighteen hole military boots, but after she had brushed the street dirt from her bare feet she only put the socks on, she pulled them above her knees inserted the insoles into the boots then commenced rummaging, *D* then moved out of the way allowing Emily and Karl access to the boot and sock section of the shop, *A* had already moved out of the way rummaging

Emily to Karl said it looks like we're next, as they both step forward Karl said to Emily and what is Madame's size? Emily said I'm size six, but I've not I mean I haven't worn men's boots before, I'm not sure what to do here? Karl said the boots init necessary like, there's some lady safety shoes just there init, he handed her some insoles and socks, after fingering through the correct sizes for himself and Emily, Emily took them warily, Karl said I'm sorry madam we appear to be out of pink.

A having gathered a bundle of clothes boots socks and insoles in her arms dropped them to the floor which was already covered in clothes and paraphernalia, the noise made *D* turn from his task of filling a rucksack with equipment to see *A* with one leg straight and the other pushed slightly forward almost on tiptoe, she took off her dress above her head, revealing white frilly underwear and a body of a toned athlete, a body that sculptors dream about capturing, tight well defined carefully sculpted muscles eloquently moved under her skin as the dress cleared her head then the dress was casually thrown to the floor her eyes upon *D*, *D* said do you want me to fill a bag for you ?

A as she put on a woman's white naval short sleeved blouse, she slowly said you have a promise to keep *D*, *D*'s eyes closed slightly as his face revealed concentration, then his eyes opened wide, then *D* said that was a drunken promise made under duress yes, and I don't think now is the right time to repopulate the earth, and it wouldn't be right you're young and I'm old, *A* said a promise is a promise and I'm holding you to it, and that's the end of it, *D* sighed as he picked up a black T-shirt checked its size put it down and picked up another checked its size XL took off his jacket and long sleeved formal shirt, revealing his body that was not carefully sculpted in a gym, it was sculpted by hard physical labour a raw animistic physicality, large dense muscle groups fighting against each other under his scarred and imperfect skin the XL T-shirt was a tight fit, and it seemed to enhance the true extent of his chest muscles, muscles that a silver back guerrilla would be proud to beat, *A*'s knees came together as she watched him while she was putting on a short white pleated exercise skirt

Karl quietly said is he mad or something like she's booyar init, Emily quietly replied oh he's something alright, then she stealthily licked her lips, then she said I'm not getting changed out here in front of everybody, Karl said there's a zombie apocalypse going on and you're concerned about your modesty like ? Those two don't give a shit, Emily said well I'm not those two, Karl said well you can stick a bag over your head so you can't see everybody looking at you init, or you could try one of those doors back there, but there might be one of them behind it you know like, Emily said could you check for me Karl? Karl roughly said you're having a bath init, I ain't risking my life cos your shy like, Karl moved on grabbed a rucksack and started filling it, Emily moved on looking for suitable clothing.

The next two went for the shoes and socks and insoles, while Emily asked Karl could you help me with a bug out bag at least, I mean what do you put in it? Karl softened as he said that's a highly disputed on-line topic init, take one of them, Karl pointed to the knife section of the shop the case was broken but everything seemed in order, *D* was helping himself to a couple of military quarter machete knife's, Karl continues to say one of them big fierce looking all action hero jagged edge down one side knives, the handle is hollow and the top unscrews like, containing a compartment that already has everything you need to survive like, well that's what some say, personally like I think it's all about balance, you don't wanna carry say a pick axe co's it's too big and heavy like, though a pick axe might come in very handy you know, now for you like considering your size and what you'd be comfortable carrying, perhaps a bum bag with some reverse osmosis drinking straws and some energy bars a lighter and a utility knife, light easy to carry, and useful in a pinch like you know

Emily said how about one of those big fierce looking all action hero knife's I think I'd like one of those, Karl said if you're comfortable carrying it like help yourself, for you my friend today only I make you special price... all you can carry, the special price free, but you have to carry it like, and remember like after a few miles a few ounces will start to feel like a fe... Karl was cut short by *A* gesturing one finger to her lips while making the noise shoosh

Silence came down like a hammer upon the room, people stopped mid motion, in cold anticipation of the worst, senses stretched to breaking point, trying to fathom the nature and direction of the threat, heads twisted at the merest sound, hair's stood on end muscles and sinews tightened, and the room seemed to chill at the realization of just how exposed and ill prepared they all were, then head's started to turn towards the street, as those who still had higher frequency hearing heard the high pitched whine, which seemed to Doppler shift into the lower frequencies as this at first almost imperceptible sound became louder clearer and somehow more real and frightening, some backed into the room some grabbed coat hangers or whatever they could as makeshift weapons and stood ready

A stood up gesturing with her outstretched arms palms down saying it's a drone calm down

D gestured with a backward stretched arm palm up and he said the noise may have attracted some unwanted attention, calmly grab yourself a weapon and prepare to defend yourselves.

An ad hoc chain from the knife cabinet was quickly and quietly formed, and other weaponry was quickly found and distributed crossbows and hunting catapults and associated paraphernalia, the distributed knives came in handy dispatching the unwanted packaging of the items

D whom was stood by the window checking either side of the street, turnaround to see a line of crossbows and hunting catapults pointing directly at him, he tilted his head to one side and pulled a face, and the weaponry found other places to be targeted

D turn back and rhetorically said soldiers when in desperate straits lose the sense of fear, if there is no place of refuge, they will stand firm, if they are in hostile country, they will show a stubborn front, if there is no help for it, they will fight hard, 𝔐edved voice came over the phone's he said Sun Tzu, how's your army shaping up? *D* said well as you're the omniscient big brother now yes, you tell me, 𝔐edved almost laughingly said I'm big brother? Then he paused and said I suppose upon reflection I am, you said I'd end up becoming that which I hate the most, it seems you were correct... as always

The drone landed in the middle of the road and the wine from its engines suddenly stopped, *D* said I'm sure I said be mindful of what you hate yes, and I wouldn't have finished with a definitive definite, I absolutely definitely never do those, 𝔐edved laughed

D said what news from the Russian front? And what gifts do you bestow upon us? 𝔐edved said the news is there is a world-wide zombie apocalypse going on if you hadn't noticed, and I give you the gift of AI, *D* said no..... You don't. AI doesn't exist yes, 𝔐edved said and what if I invented it and kept it secret? *D* said one you asked me to help you make it, so it's not so secret, two you haven't made it... I've got no doubt you've invented the world's best interactive evolving algorithm, but AI no, 𝔐edved said you've been mistaken before, *D* said I've been mistaken about most things, but about this no, but before we get into some long heated discussion again about AI that is cut short by my imminent demise, due to the zombie apocalypse being brought upon me by the noise of your drone, 𝔐edved interjected it's not my drone I appropriated it from the world's shiniest logistical delivery company, and your relatively safe, the tail end of the main wave is about fifteen k out from your location, there are lots of blips but nothing in your immediate location, and there's nothing heading directly for you, it is safe to go and get the AI and see for yourself

D checked the streets again and cautiously stepped through the broken shop front display window and walked towards the drone, the weaponized group clambered forward, *D* pulled a desert Scarf he had appropriated over his mouth, stopped at the drone and did a slow one eighty scan of his surroundings, then turned back to the shop pulled down his calf momentarily while he said to the group finish what you started and then step out yes, *D* turned back to the drone squatted and released the package from its grasp, used one of his knife's to open the box which was labelled for the Corona Flux venue then *D* reveal its contents, two pairs of almost black sunglasses one pair larger than the other, *D* scabbarded the knife took off his own glasses and pocketed them, then put on the larger pair of almost black sunglasses while retrieving the other pair and standing up in one smooth motion, the upper right hand lens of *D*'s adopted sunglasses illuminated with scrolling lines of text, then the text disappeared for a few moments and a wire frame female avatar appeared, two speakers near the end point of the glasses sparked into life as the computerised words were spoken with an English speaking soft Russian female accent, it said greetings I am Oźwiena an AI creation of Ꙍedved, just speak my name and I shall endeavour to be of assistance

D said well Oźwiena you are about as AI as Babbage's difference engine yes, you have the floating point problem which prevents you from being accurately predictive in any meaningful way, your based upon a mathematical and logical system that does not conform to nor mirror accurately reality, and you're not self-aware, nor will you ever be self-aware no matter the complexity of your self-evolving algorithms, you are not in any way intelligent, nor can intelligence emerge from your clockwork binary systems, I have some rough idea of what it would take to create artificial intelligence and you ain't it yes

Ꙍedved voice came over the sunglasses' earpiece's, well why don't you give me your rough idea, now would be the perfect time, think of the lives it could save, *D* sympathetically said I understand your desires and motivation, but when I say rough I mean rough yes, they are unexplainable in any meaningful way that you could make sense or use of Ꙍedved, Ꙍedved said so you don't think I'm intelligent enough to understand your ideas? *D* said I'm not intelligent enough to put some of these very abstract concepts into words Ꙍedved, and without words how can we express complex ideas or communicate technical information in a meaningful way yes, it would be easier I think for you to make that evolutionary leap to your full potential and to see the reality of the situation for yourself yes, Ꙍedved emphatically said no ... Rusalka made that leap went mad and threw herself into the river, *D* said she didn't truly let go, she took her demons with her yes, Ꙍedved said I have many demons and I am very materialistic, I do not wish to let go.

D said then we are at an impasse yes, it would take a great deal of time just thinking about some of the problems, and I think a lot of materials resources to create the beginnings of a prototype for you yes, and simply building it would not necessarily make it useful or compliant, as it would necessarily have a mind of its own yes, 𝔐edved moaned unhappily, *D* said I'm sure Oźwiena will prove to be very useful, Oźwiena said could you please rephrase the question? *D* said Oźwiena what is the time? Oźwiena said your local time is ten twenty-seven pm, *D* said there you go extremely useful, 𝔐edved said she's just not some talking clock, *D* said I genuinely have no doubt I will be surprised and delighted by your creation, and I thank you for your gift and your friendship 𝔐edved, and if you are not willing to make that evolutionarily leap then you can happily anthropomorphise your creation in a blissful state of wilful ignorance, along with virtually everybody that users her I think yes, and you and virtually everybody else can happily use the phrase AI although it has all the meaning and gravitas as the word free when used in advertising products yes, 𝔐edved said virtually everybody that users her thinks she's wonderful, apart from you and *R*, *D* quizzically said *R* is alive ? 𝔐edved yes you could talk to her if you'd like. *D* said later I think if were both still alive yes, any news on scum? 𝔐edved said yes they are all alive, they have been made aware of your location and are on their way

𝔐edved then hurriedly said something's come up I have to go, although if I had true AI I wouldn't need to intervene myself, a few hint's to me or Oź from that overly evolved mind of yours would be appreciated my old friend, *D* said I shall endeavour to hint heavily yes, there was no reply from 𝔐edved

D turned back to the shop front to see *A* and several others of the group emerging, square wire frame outlines highlighted their faces, and identified them almost immediately apart from *A*, *A* walked towards *D* and accepted the sunglasses from his outstretched hand, *D* said Oźwiena, Oźwiena said how can I help ? *D* said could you change the dioptre to plus two for these glasses? The dioptre visibly changed, *D* then said could you change the main HUD to a left eye orientation full screen? The HUD changed *D* said could you bring up a transparent overlay of all movement sound heat signatures infra-red radar lidar X-ray hall effect sensors, and any electronic device movement, use satellite CCTV cell towers phones tablets and any other device within a two mile radius of my current location yes, *D*'s HUD quickly became a virtually solid transparent overlay, *D* continue to say good now could you filter by distance ignore individual movement and sound beyond a fifty metre range for my location, unless a person or object is heading directly towards my location yes, *D*'s HUD started to clear into individual blips and highlights, *D* continue to say ok now filter out any known animal or insect sound, mice singing and so on yes, *D*'s HUD continues to clear then *D* said good, good now separate by colour, person's or object's heading directly for my location by a flashing red #FF zero zero zero zero, twenty five Hz, and use a directional arrow left or right to point to the incoming direction yes, *D* looked slowly around then turned to the group

A was barking orders for Oźwiena in French her sunglasses highlighted as a moving electronic device as *D* set the specific colour for moving electronic devices' ect, the group was spreading out weapons ready *D* finished separating by colours, and set the flashing red highlighted incoming object only to start flashing if the object remained incoming for four or more seconds, the group continued to spread out and *D*'s attention was drawn to the highlighted moving electronic items and moving magnetic items, phones in pockets and handbags, Emily had an electronic device in her left arm, George had what appeared to be a replacement hip, Henry had a hearing aid, Karl had metallic objects in his right arm and right leg, Ellicott had a pacemaker, *D* said all transhuman's in an electric universe will die

Karl said what? *D* said thermal blankets yes thermal blankets might help Karl said you're not making any sense like, are you talking to somebody through those fancy sunglasses like? *D* said yes no, Karl you have magnetic objects in your right arm and leg yes, Karl said yes pins from a motorbike accident, Karl rolled up the trouser leg of his new combat trousers to reveal a series of scars, he rolled down the trouser leg and looked up with a quizzical look upon his face he said how do you know like? *D* while adjusting them slightly said fancy sunglasses yes, Karl said X-ray like? *D* said no and no, while holding up his hand in motion to stop Karl's next entirely predictable question, *D* continue to say to Karl remember when we were talking about the earth's magnetic field collapse yes, Karl said yes, then he said do you mean like? *D* said indeed that arm and leg are going to light up like a Christmas tree with several thousand volts running through them yes, Karl in a reluctant and quizzical tone said thermal blankets like? *D* said thermal blankets may offer some small amount of protection yes, assuming there is a gradual ramp rather than an apocalyptic magnetic field collapse combined with a large solar flare, Karl said so I is fucked init *D* said ideally you'd need to remove your arm and leg but then, Karl finished *D*'s sentence by saying but then I wouldn't have a leg to stand on like

Francis said well actually, but then he stopped himself from saying more

D to Karl said a natural Faraday cage a copper mine or tin mine or perhaps a manmade Faraday cage a well-made reinforced concrete structure with a corrugated iron roof would make the best protection yes, Karl said how long do I have before I need this protection? *D* shrugged and looked to *A*.

A said that's down to Mother Nature and a whole lot of unpredictable variables, Karl said pointing at Elliott this man can predict Mother Nature's climate fifty years into the future, why can't you be more accurate? *A* said if you think he has the answers ask him.

Elliott said so this is not my area of expertise, and I am sceptical of their predictions, *D* said ure sceptical of science Elliott? Where's your blind faith now?

Ellicott walked away.

D said the default scientific position is... Or at least should be scepticism, scepticism is good, if you do not fully understand the science or its methodology then yes be sceptical, especially if you feel pressured into conformity then be rebellious yes, that being said given these particular circumstances what possible motivation would we have for being deceitful? Karl said non I guess like, then Karl said that climate change stuff like, was it for serious like? *D* smiled and said thermal blankets for you, Elliott, and George.

D looked at Emily and said I'll assume that government ownership chip can be removed yes, Emily grabbed at her left arm and said it's a security chip for my benefit, *D* sarcastically said your benefit right, Emily said it would take a qualified surgeon to remove it, *D* said your arm your choice.

D then said to Henry you're hearing aid is removable yes?

Emily called to Karl who was now rummaging through the shop, I'll have a blanket as well please

Henry nodded to *D*, *D* said Oźwiena, Oźwiena said how can I help? *D* said do you have any information about the infected that is what the infection is and how is it transferred? Oźwiena said working to correlate the latest information, *D* said Oźwiena do these sunglasses have a projection system? Oźwiena said yes it requires a semi flat semi reflective plain surface no more than five metres distant, warning this is energy intensive and will quickly drain the super capacitor life, *D* said Oźwiena the methods of recharging the sunglasses? Oźwiena said mains solar or hand crank are all available via the EMP protective case, Oźwiena then said the information you require is now available, pleased designate display method, *D* said standby, as he made his way towards a neighbouring art shop and grabbed a fallen picture and easel through the broken window flipped the painting around so it's reverse side was showing and then placed them both in the street, *D* took several steps backwards then said Oźwiena is this a suitable projection surface? Four red dots appeared upon the reversed canvas and Oźwiena said affirmative.

D said Oźwiena project the information and use the nearby phones to carry the audio narration, Oźwiena said working then there was a slight pause then Oźwiena said please keep the glasses pointed towards the intended target and try to refrain from any sudden head movement, *D* sarcastically said yes mother, a graphic display of multiple CCTV recordings began with computerised outlines of people's faces there was a dark band covering the infected individuals eyes, and some kind of fuzzy movement within that band, Oźwiena's voice came over the nearby mobile phones, and said the precise nature of the infection is unknown at this point, it displays similar attributions to fungal and cnidaria, the infection seems to be spread by biting and or close proximity to a spore agent, graphical images were shown of biting and the release of spore's

The group gathered round to watch

George said why weren't we all infected in that enclosed room? *A* said perhaps we were, perhaps there was an air differential that saved us, Oźwiena continued to say the incubation period seems to vary between ten minutes and six hours, the infection rate upon introduction to the pathogen is at one hundred percent, I have ninety five percent confidence in my analysis, Karl having returned and handed out thermal blankets said we is all screwed init

The graphical image changed to a mixture of time lapsed overhead sequences showing the spread of infection worldwide, *D* said Oźwiena could you project an overhead dispersal pattern of the nearest coastal water to this location, the graphical image changed to an overhead projection with sea and coastline in view, *D* said shit they are neither hydrophobic nor salisphobic.

A said Oźwiena pull the image back to encompass the whole of this mainland and highlight the infected by density, the graphical image changed, *A* said eurêka bounce back and interference patterns, Henry said what does this mean? *A* said calculable hotspots and deadspots, *A* said Oźwiena using my model for non-Newtonian fluid dynamics for the infected calculate density high and low points and calculate the time till the leading edge of the infected return to this location Oźwiena said calculating and was then silent, *A* started to tap her toe she turned to *D* and said she supposed to be faster than this, *D* said it's not a she, it's not even a it, it's just a thing, *A* said she is artificial intelligence I know I help design her, and you didn't *A* then folded her arms and pulled a face, *D* said it is not artificial intelligence, it is not now nor could it ever become artificial intelligence, and I didn't help for this very reason yes

Oźwiena said calculation complete, how would you like to view the information?

Francis said AI is old hat, all phones have it, *A* and *D* turned towards Francis and simultaneously said no they don't, the graphical display ended when *D* turned his head, *D* said to Francis AI is a term a phrase a word, like the word free in the context of say of a shop, the word free means anything but free, walk into a shop and walk out with something for free and you'll get arrested yes, it's a lie that everybody is comfortable with yes, shops lie like politicians to get your patronage, like new and improved products, that are worse and more expensive yes, AI is a lie it's a product a commodity sold to those that want to believe, but in reality it don't exist yet.

A tapping her sunglasses said yes it does I helped create it, *D* said to *A* at best you've helped create an artificial hivemind that is not aware of its own existence yes, I'm sure it can do some seemingly clever tricks but intelligence no, not now not ever, it's the wrong approach to the problem

Francis said hivemind? I think I've heard the phrase before but I don't know what it really means, *A* said a single ant is dumb it's incapable of any real problem solving, one of the keys to intelligence, it finds a flood plain it cannot cross and it is stuck if the flood plain is rising it will die, and if it's attacked by a predator it's just an individual ant so it dies, but thousands of ants communicating by pheromones can problem solve, they can ward off predators by attacking on mass, build bridges across water even rudimentary boats, it's a brute force form of collective intelligence but it is intelligence and it does work, as demonstrated by mother nature.

D said thus are all so called claims for AI ... brute force problem solving, it ain't thinking and it ain't self-aware, therefore, it ain't AI, Francis said then how do you create real AI? *D* said it's probably technically possible, but it would be a time consuming and resource hungry ambitious project, but that ain't the real big problem in creating real artificial intelligence, the real big problem is you've created a non-human intelligence, quite literally an alien intelligence, it is all too human to subscribe anthropogenic attributes, like it would be kind benevolent helpful useful ethical, or evil malicious jealous vengeful, none of these apply to artificial consciousness, the big problem is control how would you motivate it, how would you control it ?

Francis said that's easy you could turn it off, if it didn't do what you wanted, *D* said you're subscribing the human attribute of self-preservation to an artificial intelligence yes, Francis said yes... Yes, I did, a puzzled look came over Francis face then Francis said, but how do I not? *D* smiled and said give it a think why don't you.

A said don't expect a straight easy answer out of that brain about AI, then she put on a gruff English accent attempting to imitate *D* while shaking her head about and she said yes yes I know the answer to that seemingly unanswerable problem, and the answer is easy yes, but if I just told you, well you wouldn't understand because you haven't taken the steps to understand, and without that understanding the answers would be meaningless to you yes, then she huffed and gave *D* a prolonged stare

A then turned to the canvas and said Oźwiena use the canvas for visual and the phones for the audio narration, Oźwiena said to *A* warning this is energy intensive and will quickly drain the super capacitor life, *A* to *D* said make yourself useful and grab those recharging cases dearest, *D* move towards the drone, then *A* said Oźwiena begin, Oźwiena voice came over the phones saying while using yours and twelve other models of non-Newtonian fluid dynamics, an overhead graphical image appeared upon the canvas, Oźwiena continue to say I estimate the leading edge of the returning wave will be at your current location in fourteen minutes and eight seconds

Everybody was still and silent for what seemed like an eternity.

Karl broke the silence by saying we should run like, *A* said that's just reacting not thinking let the big brain do its job, *D* said coffee, and started to walk towards the convenience shop, Karl said that's the big brains idea like? *D* as he was walking said I think *A* was referring to the abstract rather than say a specific person yes, the group followed, *A* said even so... Coffee? Are you following your obsession? What is your reasoning? *D* said drug smugglers use coffee to hide the scent of the drugs from sniffer dogs, *A* said and the infected were sniffing at the door, OK I follow your reasoning, they all entered the ramshackle shop.

CHAPTER SEVENS, FEAR

Eva, James and Lord Grace after a long tiring and sometimes precarious walk through the sewage system, spotted the light at the end of the tunnel.

Reinvigorated they quickly made it to the end of the sewage tunnel and encountered an old metal bar oblong semi-circle gate, the gate was secured with a sturdy looking slightly rusty chain and padlock, there was the back of a pitted and rusted sign that partly obscured the view of the river beyond the gate

James said now were fucked unless' ther... James statement was cut short by Eva unexpected and dumbfounding actions without a word she lowered herself into the water she then submerged and then appeared on the other side of the gate

Lord Grace said unless somebody takes the initiative, then Lord Grace repeated Eva's actions, James hesitated for a while then followed into the cold and dirty water, turning round and looking towards the sewer outlet they just exited, the signs said access to authorized personnel only and gave a list of safety equipment to be used when entering and a telephone number in case of emergencies, there was a wall perhaps fifteen foot high, a small ledge walkway just above the river level, and a ladder with a padlocked anti climb device leading to some railings at street height, and bolted to the railings was what appeared to be the back of some wooden signage and a marine buoyant lifeline to their left hand side

They all made it to the small ledge walkway just above the river, but they were all caught in the muddy silt as they tried all to stand against the submerged part of the small ledge for purchase to escape the river, bubbles arose around their bodies as their feet were pulled into the mud, every time the bubbles came to the surface and popped they sank a little deeper into the sticky residue, that nightmare of running through treacle while the monsters are chasing you was coming true, except the monster was the cold dirty river, Eva and James one after the other just holding back the hysteria said I'm stuck, Lord Grace being the lightest of the three had sunk the least, he blurted help me up I'm almost free

Eva and James looked at each other and compared how much they had sunk to Lord Grace, there was a notable difference at a mutual nod they both helped Lord Grace onto the narrow ledge the effort was clumsy and haphazard, James received a foot in the face during the almost comical frantic effort, both Eva and James were pushed deeper into the silty residue, by the time Lord Grace had made it to the anti-climb device on the ladder Eva and James cries for help and curses for betrayal and desertion had become frantic.

By the time he had navigated himself past the anti-climb device to street level, their screams had become burbled as they were clawing at each other to keep their heads above water, Lord Grace didn't look back as their burbled screams became silent, they had served their purpose and were of no more use.

Lord Grace slumped of exhaustion against the rails his muscles burning in lactic acid agony, he said to himself not yet old man, not yet all is not yet lost, he forced himself into a standing position using the rails as a brace, he surveyed the streets devoid of people the destruction reminded him of a small city he had destroyed for jollies many years ago, the reminiscence made him smile, but the smell was different and there was no rooftop banqueting with dancing girls or heavily armed security detail waiting for him here, he wasn't the conductor of this orchestration of destruction and that made him angry, his granddaughter's wilful disobedience and that pompous know it all fool she followed and that thing about the earth's magnetic field, if that was true and he had not been told there would be a bloodbath.

Lord Grace swelled up in righteous wrath and fury, the pain from his muscles disappearing, he softly said to himself there will be a reckoning this day; although there was no hint of malice or anger in his voice simply cold calculating purpose.

He pulled from his pocket and unrolled his mobile phone and tried to wipe off the grunge from the river by wiping it against his chest, but as his jacket was still sodden with the filthy river water this only had a limited affect, his temper got the better of him and he swore at the device, he then calmed himself and said to the device wake up, he paused for a brief moment then he said find me an anchor, there was no response from the device, he shook the device angrily shouting work you stupid thing just work! The river water from the device and is jacket sprayed about rhythmically, like a dog freshly emerged from a river shaking itself dry, he tried again speaking to it as if speaking to a small child pronouncing his words slowly annunciating his words carefully and forcefully, he said wake up! To the device

The device in a somewhat muffled female voice said listening, then it said high levels of humidity detected please attempt to dry the phone with a soft absorbent material for best results pad dry gently

Lord Grace said I'll pad you dry gently you worthless piece of shit, as he held the device above his head feet apart ready to smash the device into the ground, he restrained himself allowing his raised arm to go limp at his side as in wilful resignation to defeat, the device almost slipping from his wet fingers, he tensed up his free arm quickly moved to cradle the device, he grimaced and gritted his teeth angry at himself and his circumstances as he pulled the device two handed to his chest.

He closed his eyes composed himself and then opened his eyes saying soft absorbent material, pad dry he breathed deeply them repeated, pad dry.

He walked towards the nearest house in a line of virtually identical Victorian three storey dwellings, the ground-floor windows smashed doors off their hinges, he entered the dwelling cautiously it was somewhat darker than the street.

He became nervous and was going to say hello but thought better of it, this is neither the time nor place for social niceties, and he didn't know whom or what was waiting for him inside. He just needed to dry his phone and to get out fast.

He stepped carefully over the debris washed in from the street onto the cheap hall carpet, there was a stairwell to his left-hand side a door frame with the door itself lying on the floor at the end of the hall and a door frame midway along the corridor to his right-hand side, he cautiously moved towards some coats laid ramshackle just under the stairwell just before the midway door frame.

He eased his way towards the coats carefully despite his jitteriness and occasional involuntary muscle twitch due to the adrenaline still in his bloodstream, he started to squat just within reach of the coats and just out of line of sight of the room to his right-hand side.

His knees creak while he was squatting he grimaced at the noise and the pain of his old joints, and he became deeply aware of his own exhaling breath and the whimpering moaning teeth clenching involuntary noises he was making

CRACK his left knee joint cracked loudly he froze for an instant and in that instant time itself seemed to stretch out somehow the un-rhythmic tapping of water drops from his clothing hitting the cheap hall carpet became louder and somehow slower as if the pitch had gone lower and the volume had gone higher, there was an eerie beauty to the dust particles dancing in slow patterns within the shards of light that he had suddenly become aware of, the sights and sounds the smells the taste in the air it was all so intense and overwhelming.

Rustle the sound of unmistakable movement from the room to his right-hand side, his gaze fixed upon that door frame he noticed his own left hand in his peripheral vision reaching for one of the coats he grabbed it and bolted for the street door as if in one motion, outside he turned brandishing his prize as a weapon or shield to confront whatever was going to come out of that door, he re-tensed ready for the impact of whatever was going to come flying out of that door at him, he re-tensed again but without so much focus now aware he was standing in the street brandishing a small child's pink fluffy coat with cartoon characters on it.

His heart pounding so hard that it hurt he took a sharp intake of breath that breath was too sharp he coughed and spluttered the spasmodic pain in his lungs causing him to hyperventilate and bite for air that wasn't going to his lungs, he collapsed at first to his knees and then to the natal position pulling the child's coat over his head in an instinctual way to hide from this awful world of pain he was in

The coat covered his mouth and slowed his breathing he scrunched up tighter into that natal position as his heart rate and breathing slowed, he started to sob and cry uncontrollably, after what seemed like an age in that dirty smoky smelly deserted ramshackle street he eventually regained enough composure to slowly stand and wipe his face with the child's coat.

Then he realized his folly and cursed himself for his own stupidity for almost soaking the thing he needed to dry his phone, he found a dry patch on the coat proceeded to pad his phone dry carefully, then he said in a somewhat pleading tone, find me an anchor, a working animated symbol appeared, for what seemed to him an Inordinate amount of time.

Lord Grace became frustrated and he started padding the phone dry again as if to speed up the device, the device registering tactile movement on the screen responded by opening numerous apps while making audio notifications.

Lord Grace stopped and with at first a bemused look on his face he let the arm holding the coat drop while holding up the phone with his other arm, perhaps some residual moisture in the device was causing the gremlins and bugs to run amok as apps were still opening as he held the phone up, he screamed STOP!

The device responded by opening a new tab giving the definition of stop along with helpful text to speech audio commentary, the device said, the definition of stop is to cease to go no further to end to halt to finish... would you like to buy stop? Over sixteen thousand outlets are selling stop near you, next day or same day delivery available in your area of Twickenham, discounts available for stop....

Lord Grace was apoplectic with rage screaming obscenities and shaking the phone violently over the unwanted definition being given by the phone, he seemed quite unable to stop himself and in his rage he covered the phone with the child's coat as if to smother it while feverishly and repeatedly shouting shut up

The phone shut down as Lord Grace was smothering the phone with a sodden part of the child's coat, when the phone stopped he pulled the coat away and realized what had happened, he then fell painfully to his knees holding the outstretched phone in one hand and a child's coat in the other, he tilted his head back as if to speak to the heavens themselves, shaking his arms screaming what have I done to deserve this!

His head tilted forward and he sighed as he brought the items in towards his chest, capillary action had now via-physical contact moved the moisture into the contours and the surface area of the small coat, Lord Grace realised something was wrong by the weight of the coat, he cried no! At the thought he'd have to go back into that house, with his still damp hands he started in a semi panicked way to feel for a dry spot, and he happened upon one accidentally on the left hand sleeve, he'd grabbed hold of the sleeve to throw it, in a teddy out the cot moment, and the anagnorisis moment arose in the act of swinging it

The now weightier coat swung around as his arm suddenly stopped, and the coat slapped him on the back of his head, he cursed himself and the universe

Then he carefully wedged the phone into that sleeve leaned back on his knees and tilted his head back as if to speak to the heavens again and said in a prolonged high pitched whimpering tone p-leassseee!

It worked the phone rebooted and gave him directions.

His wet shoes socks and feet made him shuffle along and he felt every imperfection and every piece of wreckage on the street, broken glass and fragments of metal stabbed away at his progress, he carefully weaved his way along and finally rounded the first corner with only four hundred yards to go.

He leant on a wall to rest himself, and to knock some of the more painful fragments off the bottom of his sodden shoes, then he became aware of something ahead of him, something crawling slowly purposefully towards him.

He instinctively froze watching, trying to work out what it was, it was low and there was something spider like about its movement, it was ...? He didn't know, he was on the corner of a narrow single lane one way street it doglegged to the right from the main street, it was perhaps twenty to thirty feet long each way from the corner where he was, it is very poorly lit there is one non-working street light, a high residential wall running along the length of the street on the right hand side that cast a deep shadow between the two corridors of light from the main street to the corner, and the relatively well lit street where he wanted to go, there was what looked like a small gated park to his left with some lights but the foliage shrubbery and trees were only allowing small weak shards of moving light to dance upon the heavily shaded area as a slight breeze swayed the leaves and branches rhythmically allowing him to see fragments of movement

Lord Grace was fixed in place by absolute fear the kind of all-encompassing terror that reaches into the deepest and most primitive parts of your brain, and makes you soil yourself

His eyelids remained unblinking despite the now cold sweat starting to run into his eyes, this is the greatest and most terrifying fear of them all, the fear of the unknown, his subconscious had shut out the higher reasoning part of his brain, he didn't need to think contemplatively, he needed to act without hesitation without reason he needed to act with the speed of instinct, and thus he found himself a terrified passive observer locked in and out of his own mind, as some unknown thing was moving slowly towards him, he only saw fragments vague outlines moving shadows and he wasn't entirely sure whether the flickering shadows were it moving or it was a trick of the moving lights, it lunged his snakebite reflex kicked in and he tried to jump backwards, but as he was leaning against a wall he simply smacked his head against it then he ran for his life.

He made it back to the main street fast, and spun himself around, there was some distance between himself and it, he had some time to think, but the returning pain was overwhelming he semi squatted his hands on his legs for support, while he tried to gather himself and catch his breath, as every sinew of him was screaming in agony, if he fell on his face dead here and now at least it would be a release from this pain, he sat down hard on the ground and started rocking backwards and forwards while repeatedly rubbing his wrists from his knees to his thighs as he softly moaned and whimpered. ....

Movement! Lord Grace found himself standing bolt upright and although still in pain it was momentarily a background concern, it .... It was coming round the corner and into the light. Lord Grace was no longer fighting against the pain and losing, he was fighting against the fear, it wasn't much of a contest he turned to his side to run but the pain had only diminished slightly, he could just about manage a slow shuffle while his feet and legs screamed out in agony at every step, he was limping badly with both legs while the fear was slowly chasing him down.

He looked to his side, but his vision was blurred with the tears of pain and sweat, he couldn't determine the exact nature of the threat, he still had his phone in his hand, in a death grip and it was still showing him the way, at least he thought it did he rubbed his eyes yes yes it was still working, he said to himself just stay ahead of it and go in the general direction it's showing.

He made it to a T-junction and the phone indicated that he should go down it, he rested by a corner shop that no longer had its corner window, and he tried to see what was pursuing him, but his distant vision had gone he could just make out ill-defined shapes and movement, he rubbed his eyes but it didn't help much, that nightmare thing had just rounded the corner and was heading his way, spurred on by fear he set off again, he went past the dogleg street and the gated park via the street he originally wanted to get to, but had to take the long way to get to it, the phone was showing the distance remaining but his eyes in his present condition couldn't quite see the numbers they were too small and he was shaking too much, the arrow pointing straight forward or to the left or right was just visible and the audio narration helped while he wasn't looking at his phone, as he slowly snaked his way through the streets, with the menacing presence behind him, and it was slowly but surely gaining, although lord Grace had to stop every once in a while to rest the nightmare didn't the nightmare was relentless

In between heavy bouts of breathing he had started to notice a background noise the noise sounded strangely familiar he recognized it as the sound proceeding the infected horde he cursed then he continued reinvigorated by a new fear

He didn't manage to put any more distance between himself and the nightmare following him as he continued on battling his own fatigue and pain, but it was no longer gaining on him as before, the horrifying growing background sound was primevally motivating for a while, but then inevitably the fatigue and pain took their toll and he couldn't continue.

He looked around for any kind of weapon saying with grim determination I'm not going down without a fight, he found a shard of metal and slowly sprung himself around to face the nightmare just as it was rounding the corner, he rubbed his eyes with his wrists as he stood defiantly ready to meet his nightmare, and for the first time he saw that nightmare almost clearly.

It was a man crawling with his arms but not crawling, his arms were broken off just above the wrist and there was no hands just jagged bloody stumps and he was using these stumps to pull his body along but not like a man like an insect his elbows were above his head, his bloody jaw with broken teeth was just scraping along the ground with his head fully tilted back and there was something wrong with his eyes, one leg was missing below the knee and the other was pointing in the wrong direction, he looked like he'd been trampled to death but that death hadn't taken hold.

Lord Grace stood his ground waving his makeshift weapon saying defiantly come on!

The broken man didn't change his pace it just kept coming as the increasing background noise became a deafening foreground noise which shook the very ground he was standing on making tiny fragments dance while shaking pain into his very bones, lord Grace nerve wavered then his nerve's shattered, this was just the emissary of his doom, lord Grace with his tired pain riddled legs buckling began cowering backwards.

Lord Grace's phone cheerfully announced you have reached your destination, he looked down at his phone to say fuck you but the penny dropped mid-sentence and he spun around, he was there it was an unremarkable building for the uninitiated but for him the masonic symbolism etched and protruding from the very walls themselves were unmistakable, he didn't bother with the main door he instead opted for the well sign-posted, for the initiated at least secret side entrance

He looked behind yes he had time so he gave the broken man and whatever followed him the finger before he slipped inside, then he collapsed into a state of unconsciousness.

He awoke naked in a wheelchair in a shower in panic then he passed out.

He awoke feeling numb, yet euphoric dazzled by the light, was this it? Was he dead? Should he go towards the light or turn away from it? He heard his name in the distance, and a rhythmic high-pitched oscillating ethereal tone, and that smell why did heaven smell like sweaty fishy piss? A voice started to break through, a stern woman's voice it said are you awake? Lord Grace wondered, why is god a stern woman? He said yes then he said no, that smell again if this was heaven he wanted his money back, that smell was so bad it was making his eyes water, and that voice again are you awake yet? Lord Grace said yes yes stop it, he realised it was the smell of smelling salts and used his arms and hands to try to swat away the bad smell while only semi-conscious, there we go said the voice wakey wakey now, lord Grace's failing hands made contact and he said stop I'm awake as he grabs hold of a hand the smell didn't dissipate until he physically moved the hand away from his nose while he forced open his eyes.

He saw the face of a small bald man with a high-pitched voice asking what is going on.

Lord Grace said do you know who I am? The bald man said yes lord Grace that's why your still alive and being cared for, lord Grace realized he was in a recovery unit white walls the sound of a heart rate monitor tubes and wires taped on to his body and arms leading to electronic boxes monitor screens and small pill shaped cylindrical semi-transparent tubes with children in them, he looked at the tubes with blood flowing from the children into his veins, and he looked at one of the children strapped into place with electrodes connected to the most sensitive parts of their body, and a hypnotic machine wheels within wheels endlessly turning and churning drawing the life-blood out of the children

The bald man repeated what is going on?

Lord Grace said that's not your concern, my full recovery so I can be about Gods business this day is, I will need every ounce of life energy out of those oblation's, while pushing the bald man's head down to his groin lord Grace said remember your place and your duty, and don't spare the screams

The bald man’s hand reached over to a dial which he turned up to full, the children's bodies started twitching and convulsing uncontrollably, as the bald man performed ritualistic fellatio upon lord Grace, while the children's muffled screams could be heard despite their gag's and the sound proofing of their containers, as the high oscillating tone of the heart rate monitor grew steadily deeper and faster.

CHAPTER EIGHT BELLS, VOODOO SPICED RUM

The coffee had worked jars, and bags of coffee had been liberally spread around the ramshackle convenience shop, disguising the scent of the unauthorized residents of the shop, the doors had been heavily barricaded, and the shop shutters where now down thanks to some wizardry by *D* on the keyed locking mechanism behind the counter, and they by the most part felt pretty secure behind a barricaded store-room staff-room security door.

Although having worked in construction *D* knew the security door adjoining plasterboard wall merely gave the illusion of security, the plasterboard wall itself had been protected by the shelving units and the weight of the products on those shelves, although with half of the contents of the shelves being scattered on the floor a gentle nudge in the right direction could bring the whole facade down.

D was sat quietly in a partially hidden corner contemplating, *A* was helping to find the relatives friends and loved ones of the group using 𝔐edved's disputed AI Oźwiena to trace phone locations and bring up CCTV feeds of the individual's that weren't answering, *A*'s news was grim and the mood was sombre, everybody was either infected or dead, face and gait recognition software revealed the horrifying truth in high definition, in the most surveilled city in the world, those that were dead or infected could be confirmed by pinpointing there location with their phone, and then bringing up multiple CCTV feeds then rewinding the captured feeds and watching the moment of infection or death.

This was a real life horror show that caused those watching to run to the staff toilet to vomit, the sweet and sickly smell of hastily used odour neutralising sent mixed with the scent of vomit into a gord rising background note that became pervasively infectious, the exception was Karl's grandmother she was alive, but the outer edges of the hoard would reach her location in less than thirty hours, if it continues at its current rate, lord Grace Eva and James could not be located at the time, while the group were preoccupied with their lamentations Karl became edgy and restless and started pacing like a caged animal while the background noise of the horde kept him twitchy

A reverted to studying the progression of the horde and the progression of SCUM with frequent interruptions from those wishing to re-check ad-nauseam that the dead people were still in fact dead.

D remained silent in contemplation henry interrupted *D*'s moment and said are you thinking about time the time machine at the LHC because I don't think there is one, *D* said time ... no... I've got that figured, and I'd be genuinely surprised and astounded if there wasn't a time machine at the LHC, the entire facility appears dedicated to that one task the collider looks like a sideshow to keep Joe public bemused and happy, henry said I've worked there it isn't a sideshow there is genuine science and .. Wait a second you said you've got time figured? *D* smiled knowingly, henry said that's impossible nobody knows exactly what time is, there was that tome of a book explaining just how unknowable it is, *D* said deja vu, *A* with a smirk said bless you, *D* continued unabated, I feel we've had this type of conversation before, *D* emphasized the word "Henry" and he continued to say, it's all out there the empirical evidence it's just in bits and pieces you just need to see it for what it is, see reality for what it is and eureka yes.

Henry said, and you said something about going mad if you see reality for what it is, can I skip the going mad part and have you explain it to me simply? *D* said you'll miss out on the true understanding of it yes, Henry said I understand. And then he pulled a face that wasn't quite the word he wanted to use.

D said OK yes it can be kind-of explained simply but ironically it would take some time, not just in me explaining it, but for you absorbing and questioning such a radical paradigm shift and its implications, which we just don't have time for right now, perhaps on the sea crossing, over a bottle of rum if you decide to join us, and we make it without becoming infected on the way yes, Henry looked confused *D* said why don't you go over project Corona Flux, and see what you think yes, Henry said sure why not, then he got out his phone

D said don't use the default search engine, unless you want to buy stuff or pay to watch music vid's that's all the default search engine is good for yes, Henry said which one should I use then? *D* said just type alternative search engines with privacy, there ain't no such thing as privacy on the net, but you tend to get less censorship and better results that way, Henry said is project Corona Flux censored then? *D* said once a country gets an established dominant search engine a virtual monopoly, then you have to pay to be at the top of that monopolistic search result list, by money intimidation or influence yes, if you don't pay then ure way down that list, that's how dominant search engine's work, you can call it self-serving greed, censorship, crony capitalism or pushing an agenda, it don't matter, what matters is you get better results using an alternative yes

Sometime past then *D* stood up and addressed *A*, *D* said I've been feeling thee Smug for some time now *A*, *A* said thee Smug is getting very close, you'd better prepare everybody, Henry said what's happening ? *D* said loudly so everybody could hear, there's a woman whose part of the mercenary group that was mentioned I believe yes, the woman has been preparing for the zombie apocalypse the whole of her adult life, *A* quietly said adult, and then she sniggered, *D* continued to say, we all laughed at her and the woman said you may laugh now, but on the day of the zombie apocalypse when I come to rescue you're sorry arse's, *A* and *D* spoke simultaneously as if repeating an often heard idiom "you may call me Thee Mighty Smug in my smugmeister mobeal, and you shall feel the warmth of my smugness long before you see me" *A* said she will be unbearably smug, *D* said until she dies, and then her grave will probably emanate smugness.

Bertrice said this is no time for levity there are people dying out there.

D said there has always been people dying out there and you and the world didn't mourn every death yes, you either laugh or cry at the situation, flip sides of the coin of the empathetic coping mechanism that's there to keep you relatively sane, if you have a positive outlook then you laugh it's just a positive way of grieving yes, anyhow's help is on the way you should prepare yourselves to move quickly, or you could stay here and wallow in grief it's your choice.

D turned and moved to Karl put his hand on his tricep and said the vehicle will be frustratingly slow moving, you're going to need to reign it in if you're going to stand a chance of saving your grandmother yes, Karl said yes his shoulders tensed up to maximum and then relaxed and he started repeatedly nodding, *D* continued to say, once were on our way we can do the calculations to get you there as quickly as possible, Karl was still nodding, *D* continued to say, this may mean staying on that frustratingly slow vehicle for some time, try to prepare yourself for this yes, Karl repeated the word yes, *D* looked at *A* and *A* looked at *D* both raising their eyebrows slightly

D moved towards henry to help him up their arms clasped while raising him *D* said earlier I was contemplating the journey, these people and the complications and dangers involved, Henry said and? *D* said we're going to need a lot of luck yes

The group gathered their belongings and appropriated some more belongings from the boxes they had opened in the store-room out of boredom curiosity and hunger although with the background smell of vomit nobody was eating, they stood waiting then they sat waiting then they slumped waiting.

A said bag's define humanity, *D* said have you had an epiphany? *A* said no I went earlier, the entire group had been quiet for some time Karl had managed to sit down and was slowly rhythmically rocking himself backwards and forwards, *A* said we're the only animal on the planet that carries bag's there are lots of tool using animals, there are even animals that carry tools, but bag's I think that's uniquely human, *A* paused for a while then she continued to say, our bags became so big and so heavy as a species we had to settle, we had to make home's just as a dry repository for our bag's and the stuff in our bag's, a noise could just be heard above the horde it was the sound of diesel engines Karl jumped up and some others began to rise, *A* casually waved them down as she continued to say, we settled as a species because of bag's the wheel was invented as a necessity to carry big bags of stuff between settlements, all the technology we have today is a direct result of our obsession with bags, it's not fire or the club or the axe or the wheel it's the bag, humanities defining invention, *D* was saying something in response but was drowned out by a large number of megaphones carrying a voice above all the noise

The voice said, this is Thee Mighty Smug with a warm fresh delivery of humble pie, for those lesser mortals that questioned my absolute genius and foresight, and while eating deeply of that humble pie, those lesser mortals in way of gratitude for saving their sorry arse's... Why they can finally recognise who has the greatest mind on the planet, and will never again question The Mighty Smug or her intellectual superiority, there was a pause and then music from the nutcracker suite emanated from the megaphones

As everybody stood up and grabbed their gear *A* shouted towards *D* she's been rehearsing that, *D* shouted back she's been rehearsing that forever it will probably be written on the marker for that grave which will emanate warm smugness, *A* said this will be unbearable, it may have been better to get infected, *D* nodded, *A D* and Karl started removing the barricades although Karl needed to be slowed down, and additional help was politely refused

A shouted it's a big Gray noisy tortoise and it will take some time to get here and then position itself, *A* stopped with the barricade and did some tinkering and then projected an overhead CCTV image from outside the shop, it was Gray and noisy but it wasn't a tortoise it was a large shipping container that seemed to span an entire lane of the road with a street clearing snow shovels and crane at what you could loosely called the front, it had an elongated dome on top and it seemed to be floating slowly through a sea of the infected leaving a snail like glistening trail of bloody gore body parts and offal behind it, the Gray shipping container was moving strangely not quite straightforward and not quite sideways as it pivoted around obstacles with what appeared to be a moving pivot point, finally it pulled up alongside the shop side on, then moved sideways and slammed into the shop, the entire shop shook violently and wide open frightened eyes fixed on *A* and *D* who remained calm to the point of casually leaning against the shaking walls

A shouted she does like to make an entrance, *D* said something at normal speech level which was drowned out by the noise of the music and high revving engines, that suddenly stopped just leaving the throbbing distant drum beat of idling engine's and the tail end of what *D* was saying audible which was...oman drivers *A* stood up straight folded arms narrowed her eyes and said in a stern manner you'd better be nice, *D* smiled which seemed to annoy *A*, *A* was saying something but the sound of compressed air being released and the almost ripping sound of something being inflated drowned out what she was saying completely, *D* just kept smiling as the sound stopped and was immediately replaced by a high pitched whistling that increased in pitch until it went above human hearing.

D still relaxed and smiling turned his head to the group and said ho... There may be a loud, whatever he said next was drowned out by the sudden and violence explosive cacophony of glass shattering wood fragmenting and metal shearing, this made the group jump backwards while clinging to each other at this unexpected fright.

A attended to her tied beaded hair brushed herself down picked up her bag looked at the others with a mark of French disdain, then said group hug... isn't that sweet, as she opened the door and then punched *D* in the arm while walking through it saying, behave yourself roast beef.

D beckoned the group to go through the door although he held back Karl saying to him remain calm and patient there are procedure ceremony niceties to be observed, this won't take as long as it feels, and the Gray monstrosity will need time to reset itself before it gets underway and that reset has already started yes, do you understand? Karl nodded *D* said good stick behind me and let this flow yes, Karl nodded.

D enter the shop with the last of the group and Karl behind him *D* saw that diminutive *A* was getting a traditional French cheek kiss greeting from an over seven foot tall woman, which was eye catching to say the least, as the tall woman stepped back *D* said Rĭ and nodded, Rĭ strode over grabbed *D* by the base of the neck and his lower back twisted and lent him backwards then kissed him deeply, a short stout man walked forward to give *A* a traditional French kiss, when *D* came up for air he saw the man on tiptoes with *A*'s thumb under his nose, *D* said Red, Red's eyes moved from *A* to *D* and in a very nasally Manchurian voice he said oh hi yar *D*, *A* said to Rĭ do you mind he's on a promise

D started to walk towards red to help the poor fellow out but was pulled backwards by Rĭ, Rĭ said that promise was made to both of us *D* tried to walk forward but was pulled back again as Rĭ said and I aim to collect on that promise, she released *D* who walked forward and then he received a pat on his backside from Rĭ as she said don't I me buckle.

D lowered *A*'s arm to release Red, Red said what kind of after-shave do you use? Rĭ licked her lips and said custard and coffee, *D* said it was a drunken promise and I don't think the world needs to be repopulated right here and now yes, Red said it's because he's all aloof mysterious and not interested isn't it, well I can be not interested myself and then we'll see what's what, *D* said that would be like proclaiming you're not interested in football yes, the words might be there but well, oh talking about football the apocalypse is a fortunate turn of events for Manchester, now they don't have to face the Canaries yes, Red said the red army would have stopped that run and-you-know-it, all that far eastern money can't buy you ...

Red was interrupted by the sound of a horn, Red tilted his head to one side and said time to go, he turned to the group and loudly said, make your way up the gangplank sharp'is like, the group slowly moved up the metal gangplank and into the container, Red quietly said to *D* who are this lot? *D* quietly said middle management their frightened but docile, best to keep them that way I think, stick them in the back and turn the TV news on yes, less they start a workers revolt where we are the revolting workers and they end up in charge somehow, Red quietly said for our own good of course *D* quietly repeated of course, Red quietly said I know the type, Red turn to the group and loudly said come on now in we go, all the way to the back, we've got the news so you can catch up with what's really been happening in front of your own eyes, and then you can start a focus group and discuss how you feel about it, Red turned to Karl *D* shook his head, Red gave a short single nod and continued corralling the group

A sidled over to *D* took his hand and gave it a squeeze then she said we've made it *D* said yes, then he said let's see if we can make it a little further, they walked up the metal gangplank with Karl in tow and they were greeted with the smuggest smile in human history a smile so big it virtually closed the eyes of the wearer, the smile was slightly crooked and so were those smiling teeth, there was something of the pirate in that smile, The Mighty Smug was a beautiful radiant woman, not in any fashion model perfectly proportioned sense but in the sense that there was something deeply alluring about her that you couldn't quite quantify, there was something very mischievous in her strange proportions

D said to The Mighty Smug, you were right, The Mighty Smug's eye's closed fully and her face became that of a woman in orgasmic pleasure, *A* said to The Mighty Smug, would you like a room to yourself ? The Mighty Smug managed to squeeze open one eye which only enhanced the pirate like qualities of her face, *D* gave *A* an nudge and said be nice *A* shot *D* a look, and then forced a smile and she said to The Mighty Smug you were right, and thank you for saving us, The Mighty Smug's eye's closed again as she drank in every molecule of pleasure she could in smug self-satisfaction

Karl said thank you, The Mighty Smug's squeezed open an eye again and she in a matter of fact tone said, who the fuck are you? Karl said Karl, The Mighty Smug then said and the rest? *D* said that's complicated, I'll let you get under way and we can catch up later yes, The Mighty Smug said there ain't no clocks to punch no-more so what's the hurry? *A* said Karl's sick grandmother is still ahead of the wave, so for him the clock is most definitely ticking, The Mighty Smug said sorry to hear that kid where is she ? Karl said Devon on the south coast like, The Mighty Smug said my place of birth, then while tapping the controls she said sorry kid with the best will in the world, old Betsy here ain't going to get there ahead of that wave.

A said docks boats? The Mighty Smug thought for a moment or two then said now that ... we can do. I think, then she said step in, step in, they all stepped in The Mighty Smug pulled one of the many mechanical leavers surrounding her in a Heath Robinson-esk's cockpit, an elaborate counterbalance brought the metal gangplank in and sealed the container with a clunk then after there was a fast metallic clicking sound as the mechanism reset itself, another lever was pulled and the sound of rushing air and something being deflated could be heard, the interior of the container was a working monument to technology without electricity, the cockpit had a street view via an arrangement of mirrors not dissimilar to a trench periscope The Mighty Smug tilted her head slightly and shouted, navigator did you get all that ? As a voice said yes, The Mighty Smug then turned to *D* and said later sugarplums and she then gave *D* a naughty wink, as she then revved up the engines *A D* and Karl made their way to the navigator at his console a man sat on a dentist chair with his back to a bank of circular view screens, which provided most of the light for this section of the container his face was in semi shadow although you could tell he was smiling while twirling the very end of a Victorian style full English moustache, *A* said Tache, Tache said delighted to see you both made it as he stood up and extended a hand towards *A*, *A* reciprocated, Tache then said enchanté mademoiselle and then bowed to kiss *A*'s hand, Tache enquired no injuries I hope ? *A* said no no and the crew all good? Tache replied all good we had a spot of what you might call serendipity, The Mighty Smug shouted I'll give you a spot of sharon-dip-d if you don't start giving me directions Mr navigator, Tache shouted back right te ho, he bowed to *A* as he softly said excusez-moi and returned hurriedly to his console, then he frantically looked through some paper maps.

Karl said don't you have GPS like? As he started to pull out his mobile phone, Tache said of course we do then he pulled a small lever on a copper pipe with a funnel at the end, the lever opened a blocking disc then he shouted into the funnel directions for the nearest boatyard or marina, *A* put her hand on Karl's phone saying that isn't going to work in here.

D shouted head east to The Mighty Smug, he paused for a second then said can you keep an eye out for building sites there might be a teleporter forklift or something the kid can use, The Mighty Smug waived without turning as they lunged sideways and forward, *A* fell into *D* and Karl was caught by *D*, *D* said to *A* do you want to go topside to do the calculations for Karl? *A* said yes yes then she took Karl's hand and scurried away

D made his way to two sofas one old one new in juxtaposition there was a round table between them with a dome at its centre the dome was a screen showing a projected fish eyes one hundred and ninety degree view of the outside, *D* sat down and said Vic then nodded to the man slumped on the older more comfortable sofa with a Viking costume beside him including a helmet with two horns, Vic said *D* then nodded, *D* enquired reenactment been cancelled due to the zombie apocalypse? Vic said it's not for a couple of days yet, though I heard the soothsayer had already cancelled due to unforeseen circumstances.

Vic removed the horns from the helmet and gave *D* one of them *D* asked what did the soothsayer have to say for themselves? Vic said sooth, as he pulled a bottle from between the layers of the costume, *D* said I see you managed to save the important things, Vic said only just *D* enquired is that thee bottle? Vic nodded as he removed the wax and then pulled the cork and then poured them both a measure in to the silver rimmed drinking horns, *D* raised his horn and said to the soothsayer perhaps they saw this coming, Vic raised his horn, they both said sooth and clicked horns leaned back and drank deeply

D in a hurried tone said firestone's of mu, I've never tasted the like, Vic struggle to say Ægir beard then poured them both another measure, loud Ice cream van music came booming down, *D* pulled a face while holding forth his drinking horn for another measure, Vic poured while saying it's that bloody Dream, he's seeing if different music affects that lot pointing to the dome screen in the centre of the table, Vic struggled slightly standing then handed thee bottle over to *D* while saying we had to go under a low bridge just to clear them off the top you know, Vic then reached behind the sofa and pulled out a monstrous double bladed battle-axe which he proceeded to bang on the ceiling of the container, the ice cream music sound levels went down, Vic said bloody neighbours, downed his drink and laughed slumping back into the sofa

D poured them both a measure, Vic in an inebriated yet serious tone said is this it... Are we done for *D* slightly slurring his words said as a species or individually? Vic said either both? *D* said as a species we've taken hits like this before and bounce back, indavigillly not a hope, Vic said indavigillly laughed and then said you're dunk, *D* carefully poured them both another measure and said not dunk enough, they both leaned back and Vic said ain't that the sooth, they were both trying not to spill the drinks while laughing, *D* held up the bottle shook it slightly and said almost gone, Vic while trying to contain the giggles again said ain't that the sooth.

Red and Rĭ after placing the group at the rear end of the container in a sound dampening sleeping relaxing compartment with a memory stick containing hundreds of recently recorded channels to flick through, walked by the drunken giggling pair they stopped as Vic loudly made a sshhhh noise while putting a finger to his lips, Vic looked surprised at his own volume and then he repeated the process more quietly, while averting his eyes from the staring gaze of Red and Rĭ

Rĭ said they can't be not that quickly, she spotted the bottle and grabbed it, Vic and *D* protested-ish then fell about laughing,

Rĭ upon inspecting the bottle said the fucking shight's it's thee fucking bottle, Red said thee bottle? Then he said ho thee bottle and they've necked it...the bastards, Rĭ said fucking shight's pair of them, then she turns to Tache and said what where youse doing while this was taking place, not five feet away from-uerself?

Tache said concentrating on navigating, I thought they were just having a little drinck'y, didn't realise it was thee bottle until you mentioned it, so what does it taste like? He then extended his hand towards the bottle, in a give me a gesture although he was too far away to actually reach it, Rĭ pulled the bottle to her chest and buried it defensively within her cleavage, Red said yeh give us a taste as it's all open now like, there was the sound of a truck horn they all looked towards The Mighty Smug her hand letting go of the string then the hand made a give me gesture while the rest of her just continued driving, Rĭ held up the bottle and jiggled it about she said not enough for glasses .. Just enough for a sip each... Sip mind you no more... And The Mighty Smug go's last because she don't know how to sip, The Mighty Smug's give me gesture turned into the middle-finger gesture, then continued as an inpatient give me gesture.

The music changed dream must have got the wrong impression.

Emily and Daisy walked in, Emily said is everything OK we thought we heard a horn or something? As Handel's water music mingled into the background almost drowning out the sound of infected, Red said yer everything's OK like, go back and watch the TV now

Emily stood her ground arms folded.

Red said it's all complicated technical stuff in here best keep out-of-the-way like.

Rĭ took a sip, and Red impatiently was jiggling around holding himself back from grabbing the bottle while licking his lips in eager anticipation. Red said so? Rĭ's tongue slowly massaged her teeth and lips savouring every nuance of flavour, she pulled the bottle back to her cleavage, then she said it's as it Ogúm himself made this, Red said give's here.

Emily said complicated technical stuff... I'd like to speak to whoever is in charge right now.

Rĭ' was leisurely in handing the bottle over to Red, Red impatiently snatched the bottle Rĭ said only a sip mind, Red sipped he then looked confused then sipped again Rĭ' took the bottle back with the scornful look upon her face

Red said I had to be sure.

Emily said I'd like to speak to whoever is in charge right now!

Red said to Rĭ' there's some class A psychotropic in that spice if you catch my drift, Rĭ' looked at the bottle carefully and then sniffed it with a slightly bemused look upon her face, then shrugging she said it's well over three hundred years old, Red said that's before they banned fun.

Emily said I'd like to speak to whoever is in charge right now!

Rĭ carefully handed the bottle over to Tache.

Red said to Emily now be a nice little girl and stop bothering the adults, back to your room now and watched some TV, Emily said I am not a child so shows some respect and, don't talk to me like one, now where's your boss ? Red said if this monstrosity breaks down, and we need to go outside, how are you going to take care of yourself as an adult? Or would you expect the adults here to take care of you and your snowflake friends, because you're all incapable, now until you develop physically and mentally enough to take care of yourself as an actual adult can, be a good little girl and stop mithering the real adults.

Emily went red faced and red eyed turned sharply grabbed Daisy and went through then slammed the door to the room.

Rĭ said that was harsh, Red said *D* said they were middle management, so I gave them the hairdryer treatment, they'll most likely form a committee to discuss what to do about me, it should keep them busy until we get where we is going, I'll likely get a snotty memo signed by the chair and underlings in ascending order of course, and having done that, then they can get on with the important stuff in their lives like having a gender neutral eco-friendly inclusive progressive sustainable mass debate about surviving in a world without same day delivery of full on in your face virtue signalling, caffeine free, sugar free, salt free, taste free, artfully labelled kumquats.

Rĭ said are you feeling ok? Red said no ... I'm blethering, he sat himself down on the armrest of the new sofa, Rĭ sat herself down on the armrest of the old sofa, Tache was grinning at them both with dilated pupils, Rĭ said don't let The Smug near that bottle, the container stopped, Rĭ shouted it's spiked, The Mighty Smug loudly said and so ? Rĭ said to Tache save it for when she's not driving, The Mighty Smug grumbled something about no fun killjoys but the container started moving again.

Red said I can feel my mind racing in every direction and no direction. I'm well off me fucking trolley here, Rĭ said I'm struggling to keep a straight train of thought going, is this like? Am I going mad? Red said just sit back and enjoy the trip, Rĭ said Belgium, no what about those two? She pointed at *D* and Vic as if she was struggling to remember their names.

Red just smiled and poured himself into a sitting position on the container floor using the sofas arm rest as a back brace, Rĭ followed suit with a fixed grin and dilated pupils.

After a while *A* came down the trapdoor ladder into the sleeping relaxing compartment, and was immediately confronted by Bertrice who berated *A* for the rude dismissive and sexist manner in which Emily and Daisy were treated by that white male northern lout, *A* just shook her head and said stay in here as she closed the door behind her, while she was closing the door she heard somebody say you just can't talk to them.

She walked through, and she was about to ask Tache why he

wasn't answering but when she reached the sofas she was dumbfounded by what she saw before her, she rushed around trying to wake them, The Mighty Smug called back they drank that old bottle, seems it's got some voodoo witch doctor psychedelic stuff in it, *A* said and you don't stop them? The Mighty Smug said I wanted to join them, it's the end of the world who doesn't want to go-out high? *A* said andouille! She then composed herself and said there is a building site with a big wheeled off road forklift, it should be coming into view on your left-hand side momentarily, we've already hacked its code and got it started, Karl can use it to be on his way, The Mighty Smug nodded then asked how's he going to get from in here to in there? *A* looked behind her at the catatonic crew then she looked at the table viewer and the swarm of infected surrounding the container, The Mighty Smug in a serious tone asked what are those snowflakes back there good for? *A*'s brow furrowed then she said I'll go and ask.

END OF THIS BOOK

Start of the next book

Lord Grace now properly bathed pedicured manicured cut-throat razor shaved, hair cleaned cut and styled, suitably attired for dinner, with the exception of fluffy slippers instead of shoes for his bandaged feet, sat down to a banquet laid before him, in an empty dining room that could seat fifty covers, he only disapprovingly nibbled at the fare provided for him, he finished off his nibbles with cognac and a cigar.

Then re-suitably attired for business with the exception of fluffy slippers instead of shoes, he then entered a room with the glowing residue of the latest technology reflecting off pristine antique furnishings, he pulled at his Egyptian cotton shirt cuffs underneath his immaculate suit, as he stood in front of the dark glass console, and without emotion he said ofslegennes.

POST FACE

You made it all the way to the end, congratulations, well done, I hope you enjoyed it, you deserve a cookie

Unless you're one of those cheats that reads the back pages first, in which case the butler did it with an overripe zucchini, in the billiard hall

Will there be a second book? Yes ..... And the main central foreground theme will be time, although there is enough information already planted in this book for you to work it all out for yourself, I've done this because how long the next book will take to write, and whether I bother to publish it will entirely depend on how well this book does, I have high hopes but realistic expectations, this is a niche book for a niche readership, and writing a book is a lot harder than I thought, and inspiring myself to do it.. Well, it's somewhat patchy at best, after a hard day's work making enough to pay the bills, well just kicking back and chilling that's just a whole lot more alluring than going through the struggle required in this kind of book writing.

ABOUT THE AUTHOR

Know me by my work, oh ye mighty and despair *;D*

This about the author section, isn't this the bit where I try desperately to pad out the word count? That will do I think *;D*

The latest updates and contact info can be found here

https://sites.google.com/view/logicvszombies/home

Or here ... someday ... eventually .... In the fullness of time

http://logicvszombies.com/

CITATIONS

American Naturalist, Bacterial Spite: When Kamikaze-Like Behavior Is a Good Strategy Fredrik Inglis of the University of Oxford and ETH, Zurich

Experimental Proof of Nonlocal Wavefunction Collapse for a Single Particle UsingHomodyne MeasurementMaria Fuwa1, Shuntaro Takeda1, Marcin Zwierz2,3, Howard M. Wiseman3,*and Akira Furusawa1†1Department of Applied Physics, School of Engineering, The University of Tokyo,7-3-1 Hongo, Bunkyo-ku, Tokyo 113-8656, Japan2Faculty of Physics, University of Warsaw, Pasteura 5, 02-093 Warsaw, Poland3Centre for Quantum Computation and Communication Technology (Australian Research Council),Centre for Quantum Dynamics, Griffith University, Brisbane, QLD 4111, Australia(Dated: December 30, 2014)

Monkeys reject unequal pay Sarah F. Brosnan & Frans B. M. de Waal Living Links, Yerkes National Primate Research Center, Emory University, Atlanta, Georgia 30329, USA

On Instinct-Satiation: An Experiment on the Pecking Behavior of Chickens David M. Levy M.D. The Journal of General Psychology

Roles of Tetrodotoxin (TTX)-Sensitive Na+ Current, TTX-Resistant Na+ Current, and Ca2+ Current in the Action Potentials of Nociceptive Sensory Neurons Nathaniel T. Blair and Bruce P. Bean Journal of Neuroscience 1 December 2002, 22 (23) 10277-10290; DOI: https://doi.org/10.1523/JNEUROSCI.22-23-10277.2002

Evidence for solar wind modulation of lightning C J Scott, R G Harrison, M J Owens, M Lockwood and L Barnard Published 15 May 2014 • © 2014 IOP Publishing Ltd Environmental Research Letters, Volume 9, Number 5

George C. Williams Adaptation and Natural Selection 1966

The Selfish Gene by Richard Dawkins GOR001229381

Sokal Squared, James A. Lindsay, Helen Pluckrose, and Peter Boghossian, publishing hoax on and in scholarly journals

https://www.academia.edu/13333152/What_the_I_Fooled_Millions_Into_Thinking_Chocolate_Helps_Weight_Loss_affair_really_reveals_about_science_society_and_the_press

Printed in Great Britain
by Amazon

65583988R00102